Callahan Goes South

ALSO BY FRANCIS H. AMES

THAT CALLAHAN SPUNK
THE CALLAHANS' GAMBLE

Callahan Goes South

FRANCIS H. AMES

DOUBLEDAY & COMPANY, INC.

GARDEN CITY, NEW YORK

1976

All of the characters in this book
are purely fictional, and any resemblance
to actual persons, living or dead, is coincidental.

Library of Congress Cataloging in Publication Data

Ames, Francis H
  Callahan goes south.

  I. Title.
PZ4.A5Caj [PS3551.M4]   813'.5'4
ISBN 0-385-11262-9
Library of Congress Catalog Card Number 75-36577

*This book is dedicated to my
vivacious niece Elaine Ames Thieman*

Callahan Goes South

CHAPTER ONE

After we had returned from the Big Cougar River country in the fall of 1914, driving a herd of cattle that Bill Bullow of the Lucky Horseshoe outfit had bought from Clem Scott of the Z Bar O, we put in a fairly mild winter, that is, for Montana. This meant that we didn't have many days when it went down to more than forty degrees below zero and not too many three- and four-day-long blizzards.

We had taken in sixty head of Bill Bullow's cows to winter for half the calf crop, because we had plenty of hay, having had to cut our grain crop in the fall of 1914 for fodder because it had been beaten flat by a heavy hail storm before we could harvest it for threshing. We wintered well and after turning the herd out on the open range and putting in the grain crop, we faced the more-or-less easy days of late spring and summer.

Ever since we had made the trip south from Coyote Wells to the Big Cougar River country I couldn't get my mind off of the area through which we had passed. Here, where we lived now, the land was gently rolling, saged and buffalo-grassed prairie, without trees or running streams. It was hard to believe that only a few miles south lay a far different country, where trees grew and water ran, and where there were still miles of open range. The only water we had, since Sam Purcell had fenced off the Beaver Creek railroad section to the south of the homestead, was the two-mile stretch of alkalied potholes of Bonepile Creek. But far to the south ran the Elk, the Box Gulch, and the Little and Big Cougar rivers.

I was thinking, and Pa knew it, of going down there and either filing on surveyed government land or squatting on unsurveyed sections, and holding the latter under squatter's right until it was surveyed. Pa kept reminding me that, being only nineteen years old, I was too young to file on land, even though I now stood nigh to six feet tall and weighed a hundred and eighty pounds with my boots off. I kept reminding him that we now had too large a herd of cattle and horses for the range we controlled and that we simply had to get more range or sell off our newly acquired, fine-blooded breeding stock. I was mulling all this over in my mind when we got a letter from Massachusetts, informing us that Mother's sister, Ina, had died.

This was a great shock to us all, but we were pleased when Aunt Ina's husband, my uncle Pete, sent another letter, telling us that he had sold his forty-acre farm, and since he was now all alone and lonely, he was going to visit us, and expected to settle down near us. Since Uncle Pete had been my favorite relative when we lived near him in Massachusetts, I found myself looking forward to his arrival. Thinking about this, it occurred to me that I didn't really know much about Uncle Pete. I was only a twelve-year-old kid when I had last seen him, in 1908, and now I was a man grown.

"What's Uncle Pete like?" I asked Pa. "You knew him when you were just kids together."

Pa's round, florid face lit up with glee, and his mustache started to twitch the way it does when he is feeling tickled about something. Ma, turning from the stove, noticed this right away.

"Now, John," she warned, "don't you go to making up any of your stories about my brother-in-law. Pete is a nice man."

"Making up stories!" Pa echoed, his features now as innocent-appearing as a newborn baby's. "Now, Trix, you know as well as I do that a person doesn't have to make up stories about Pete. All a person has to do is stick to the out-and-out truth."

"And," Ma said acidly, "just what do you mean by that?"

"Well," Pa said, "you'll have to admit that he was a mite peculiar, even as a kid."

"When he arrives," Ma declared, "he won't be the only peculiar person around this ranch. I know of somebody else . . ."

"Let's you and me," Pa said hastily as he went out the door, "go down to the barn and see if the horses are all right."

When we got to the barn, Filly, my strawberry-roan saddle mare, whinnied at me, and I went to stroke her sleek neck.

"What do you really mean," I asked, "about Uncle Pete being peculiar? He was my favorite relative. When we stayed at his place when you were out here getting the homestead ready for us to come to it, he furnished the cartridges for my .22 rifle and paid me ten cents apiece for every woodchuck I killed on his farm. I recall him as a little, jolly man, with real bushy eyebrows and a red, walrus mustache."

"And," Pa said, "a red face. Always had a keg of hard cider in the cellar. Sampled it often, he did. He's a thick-headed Welshman—his folks were born over in the old country. I wonder what he thinks this Montana country is like. He'll be fit to be tied when he gets here and finds that there ain't ary apple tree within a hundred miles. I wouldn't be at all surprised if your uncle Pete don't take one good look around the horizon and leap back on the steam cars like his tail was afire. Feller like him is mighty apt to act impetuouslike."

Pa dug out his pipe and thoughtfully tamped the bowl with tobacco, hoisted a leg to scratch a match on the seat of his trousers, lit the pipe, and puffed contentedly.

"Your uncle Pete," he said finally, "is a hard man to tack

down, build a corral around. Knew him well as kid and man—you see, we courted and married sisters. But he was a mite peculiar."

"How peculiar?"

"Well," Pa said, "for instance, he had a strong hankerin' to fish. Did it, too."

"What's peculiar about that? I like to fish too. But around here there isn't any fishing water—that is, this side of the Box Gulch Creek, and it's two days' ride south."

"And that," Pa said, "is just the point. There wasn't any fishing water either where we were raised as kids. But Pete fished anyway."

"Without water," I crowed. "How'd he do it?"

"Off the top of the barn and in the pigpen," Pa declared. "He would sit on top of the barn with a long pole and a length of line, baited with a piece of bacon rind. He'd dangle that around among the chickens strolling around below, until one of them grabbed the bacon rind. Then he'd hoist the critter, lickety cackle, feathers flying, before it could let go. Sometimes he did this so fast that the chicken got hauled clear to the top of the barn before it could let go. But mostly they'd let go halfway up and go flying all over the yard, squalling to beat the cards. The old rooster didn't like this one bit. He'd strut around, cackling and rattling his spurs, looking for something or other to jump onto about the affair. Pete would stand up there on the barn roof and laugh fit to bust."

"I see," I said.

"Never did the chickens no harm," Pa went on, "I guess. Thinking back on it, they seemed to sort of like it. Broke up the monotony of the day, one might say. Hogs liked it, too."

"Hogs?" I queried.

"Yeah," Pa said. "Did the same thing with the hogs."

"Bosh," I said. "A person couldn't dangle a bacon rind before a hog and then flip it into the air when it took it."

"Didn't say nothin' about flip, did I, boy? Drawed would

be more like it. He let the hog swaller the bacon rind, clean down into its belly, and then he slowly drawed it out again. Porker's eyes sort of bulged when he did this. Tickled Pete to death. Far as he was concerned he was fishing, and as far as the hog was concerned it was enjoying eating pork rind after pork rind. Never seemed to get wise that it was always the same rind, over and over. Down it would go, up it would come, and down it would go again. Never saw nothin' like it and neither did anyone else. Peculiar, like I said. Pete always said what a blessing it would be if a person could eat his lollipop over and over that way. I imagine that he went around trying to figure out a way to invent a re-eatable lollipop. Always tryin' to invent things, your uncle Pete was. Never did, though, to my knowledge, anything that would work, anyhow."

"I remember," I said, "that he did take me fishing a couple of times when I was there on his farm. But there didn't seem to be any fish in that creek there."

"Recall that creek," Pa said. "Back East they call them brooks, not creeks. Pete never got over buying a farm with a brook on it that didn't have ary fish in it. I reckon that if he ever found water with fish in it he'd be fit to be tied."

When Pa said that, I found myself thinking of those big catfish Pa had heaved out of the Box Gulch Creek when we were down there on the cattle drive for Bill Bullow. My thoughts took me back to our camp that night on Elk River, with the rustle of leaves under Filly's hooves, the evening-muted sound of running water, and how I had lain down on my belly and thrust my face into the stream to drink. I recalled the sweet scent of Shagnasty's campfire as I'd lain in my bedroll, listening to Filly feeding on the lush grass, and looking up, watching the moon thrust silvery fingers down through the lacery of cottonwood and box-elder boughs overhead, while a southbound flock of geese sent down their goodbye call to the north and the fast-approaching winter. In my mind's eye I could picture being there again, and maybe owning a section of that land for my very own.

"Pa," I said, "since Uncle Pete wrote that he wanted land out here, maybe he'd like land along the Box Gulch, or the Little or Big Cougar rivers. I could go down there with him and show him the way and maybe we could take Shagnasty Smith along, too. You see . . ."

"I see," Pa said wearily. "You ain't never got the idea out'n your head about taking up government land down there. Well, in the first place, all of it ain't been surveyed yet. In the second place, you ain't twenty-one years old yet— too young to file on government land. In the third place . . ."

"In the third place," I interrupted, "a person can file on land, even if he isn't twenty-one years old, if he is the head of a family."

"Right," Pa said, "and as far as I can figure out, I'm the head of this family, and will be for quite a spell."

"But," I countered, "I'll be the legal head of a family once I get married."

"Married!" Pa exploded, blowing down the stem of his pipe and scattering sparks and ashes about.

"Harrumph!" he growled, brushing off the ashes and stamping on the sparks. "You and that Joan Bauer girl, eh. Gone that far, has it?"

"Well," I hedged, "I ain't exactly got around to asking her yet. A person don't get much time to get a girl off alone during a Montana winter. And then she's been kind of standoffish ever since we had the battle with Jed Dupre and Steve Holden and their three rustler chums."

"Standoffish?" Pa queried.

"Yes," I said. "She knows that Jed Dupre stole our heifers because he was so mad at me for going with her, and she is afraid that Jed will do something else to hurt us if she continues to see me."

"You going to ask her?" Pa queried. "Or are you afeard to?"

"I'm going to ask her," I said. "Right soon."

"Don't hardly seem right," Pa said. "You being only nineteen."

"You were only eighteen when you started courting Ma."

"I guess I was," Pa admitted, "but it seems like I was older, now I look back on it. And then, your ma took considerable courting time before she said yes. There was this feller, George Simpson, with the waxed mustaches and the squint, carrying a bunch of posies. I skeedaddled him out of there in no time, with a black eye, scatterin' posies with every jump."

Pa's blue eyes gleamed with humor as his thoughts drifted back to his courting days. And then he turned to me and laid a huge hand on my shoulder, the big fingers slowly increasing their pressure until they hurt as they dug into my flesh.

"Boy," he said, "if you want this Bauer girl. If you really want her, like I did your ma when I was your age. If you're sure. You just wade in there and get her. Don't take any no's for answers. Some of these females have to be sort of crowded up agen the corral fence."

I knew that Pa was thinking of mares, and our big stallion, Bell Boy, not girls, when he spoke of crowding against corral fences. But just the same, what he said gave me a wonderful feeling, because what he was really saying was that he would welcome Joan Bauer into the family if I was lucky enough to get her. I felt like I was walking on air.

"But that idea you have," Pa went on, dropping his hand from my shoulder, "of taking Pete down into the Box Gulch and Big and Little Cougar country is foolishment. Like taking a preacher into a cathouse—he wouldn't likely fit in to the picture, you might say."

"Why not?"

"Pete," Pa said, "is used to farming forty acres with a

one-horse cultivator, mowing machine, and hay rake. He never rode a horse in his life and he ain't never been more'n a mile from a trolley car into town. Stick him into a Sentinal Butte saddle, and drop him into that wild country down there fifty to a hundred miles from civilization, and it would be murder."

"You," I said, "were farming twenty acres with one horse when you came out here."

"Me," Pa declared, "and your uncle Pete are entirely different critters—he's damned peculiar."

And, I thought, as I tossed my saddle on Filly, Ma says that you are peculiar, but it is that very peculiarity which makes her, and me, love you. And probably it is Uncle Pete's so-called peculiarity which made him my favorite relative when I was a kid. But when I had led Filly out of the barn and mounted her I stopped thinking about Pa and Uncle Pete and began thinking about a slim, dark-haired, brown-eyed girl in Coyote Wells, who moved with the grace of a thoroughbred.

As I rode west it came to me that the country hadn't changed much during the seven years we'd been here. Sam Purcell had rented and fenced in the section south of us from the railroad. This shut us off from the Beaver Creek water and range and produced a lane of fencing down to our southwest corner post. The government land lying immediately west of Purcell's railroad section was once more open range, because the Turner family had given up the struggle, as well they might, not even being able to get well water on this homestead, and most of it consisting of a barren prairie-dog village. Since we had leased the railroad section lying to our immediate west, and the one beyond the Bonepile Flats, we had water and an additional 1,280 acres under our control, besides what poor graze we got on the flats themselves. In the past, somebody had filed on the Bonepile Flats, it being open to homestead, but had quickly

starved out, leaving behind only a now-honed-down sod
shanty and a breaking plow rusting in the weather.

People had come, even as Pa had said that they would,
but as the banker, Hardwick, had predicted when I had
gone to him to see him about a loan, few had made a go of
it. Some had stuck it out long enough to prove up on
their claims so that they could sell out to some prosperous
rancher, anxious to get more graze, or to persons of wealth,
such as George Dupre, Jed Dupre's saloonkeeper father.
Others had just up and left, weary, beaten people.

We were here yet because, with the two railroad sections
under lease, the Bonepile Flats sandwiched in between
them, we had over sixteen hundred acres at least partially
under our control, and the water of the Bonepile Creek.
And—and this was of most importance—we had Bill Bullow
for a friend and neighbor. He had reached out a helping
hand the fall previous, to save us from utter disaster, when
we could have lost the homestead and everything else with
it. Hardwick, the Coyote Wells banker, had quoted John
Wesley Powell, director of the United States Geological
Survey, as saying that in this country a person had to have
at least four sections, or twenty-five hundred acres, to sur-
vive. The only place I knew of where I could have that
much range to graze over was to the south.

On our trip south we had seen open country stretching
from the Breckenridge place on Elk Creek, some twenty
miles south of Coyote Wells, to the rough country bordering
the valley of the Big Cougar River, where we had encountered a herd of sheep, which was unfenced and as wild as it
was in the days of Sitting Bull and Crazy Horse. Here I
could take up 640 acres, a whole section, under the Grazing
Act, in an area which might be poorer land for the farmer
but was ideal for the cattleman, with trees and running
water and sheltered coulees lush with native bunch and
buffalo grass.

I recalled Bill Bullow's telling us that this area had once

been prosperous cattle country, but the herds had been wiped out in the winter of 1886–87, when even Teddy Roosevelt and the Marquis de Mores had decided that they'd had enough and quit. But these cattlemen, I told myself, were men of the old school, the school that let them range like buffalo, to live or die according to the odds of the weather. It could be done differently, I thought, so that a person could pull cattle through even if we again had such a bad winter as 1886–87 had been. The old-timers didn't put up hay, plant gardens, milk cows, keep chickens, have butter and eggs. I would. They ran too many head to properly care for them. They ran a longhorn breed, standing tails to the bitter winter winds, perhaps driven up from the warm winter country of Texas, not hardened to forty below. In this way they had met disaster.

I'd thought a lot about this, dreamt my dreams about it, and in those dreams, part and parcel of those dreams, was Joan Bauer, maid to the Preston family in Coyote Wells. Without her, I knew, my plans to become a big rancher in the south country would fly up and slap me in the face. I wondered what Joan's reaction to all this would be. It seemed to me to be one thing to have a girl let you kiss her, and quite another to ask her to bed down with you for the rest of her life. The Prestons had a fine house, with indoor plumbing, and I'd had a peek into Joan's room there, and it had a real carpet on the floor, and lace curtains, with silky-looking covers on the bed. A girl would be foolish, it seemed to me, to leave such a place to go fifty or more miles into the wilderness to live in a log cabin hunkered against a coulee bank to break the wind. Thinking about this, I came near to turning Filly back toward the homestead. But then I thought that I'd just ride in and call on Joan and keep my mouth shut about what I had on my mind.

Looking back, it had been just about a year ago that I'd ridden into Coyote Wells, on a day like this, with white, fine-weather clouds scudding across the sky, throwing fast-moving shadows on the prairie floor, with now and then a thin scatter of raindrops, bringing a tang to the air and gleaming in the sun like jewels on the blades of spring grass. On that day a year back, I had first seen Joan, picking flowers in Prestons' yard, and asked her to go to the Starvation Flats dance with me, and darn near fell out of my saddle when she agreed to go. And here I was again riding into Coyote Wells, and this time with a yearning to ask a far more important question, and without the courage to do it.

I rode on, thinking about courage, and of Pa, and his Callahan blood, which he claimed he inherited from his Irish grandmother and which was supposed to rise up in a person's arteries in an emergency and get a person out of a bind. At such times Pa was inclined to call himself Callahan, though of course his real name was Conway. Folks that he was mad at at the moment were always puzzled no end by this. And here, I thought, is the core of the matter. Pa's Callahan blood, and any of the wild fluid I had inherited from him, didn't ever seem to rise up and help a fellow out unless we were mad. In the past, when my blood had seemed to rise up and make me stronger I had always been mad, like the time Jed Dupre had called me out of the dancehall and challenged me to fight. I'd gotten mad then and found the strength in me to knock Jed down. But I wasn't mad now. I was in love. And, by cracky, that was an entirely different matter. I didn't reckon that my Callahan blood was going to do me a bit of good when it came to facing Joan Bauer and asking her to marry me. I rode on down toward the Bonepile Flats, with the idea of looking over our herd before going on into town.

CHAPTER TWO

I turned off of the Coyote Wells trace and rode up on the end of the ridge where I could overlook the Bonepile Flats. Our stock was scattered below me, grazing here and there on the lush spring grass. It was a far different herd now from what it had been in past years. There were about fifty head of spring calves, some from our own inferior cows, twenty from the heifers Bullow had given us for driving the Z Bar O stock north the previous fall, and twenty-five from our share of the calf crop we'd earned for wintering sixty head of Bill Bullow's cows. These cows were still with our herd but would be cut out as soon as their calves were old enough to wean. This mixture of animals made up over a hundred head, one hundred of which, calves and all, were ours. Since we did not and could not control the grazing rights of the Bonepile Flats, a mile of it being homestead land, stock other than ours and Bullow's sometimes watered and grazed here. This was far too much stock for the area to handle, even now. When our herd increased it would be totally inadequate.

I sat there on Filly, thinking about it. There was no way that we could get more pasture land. We had reached our limit here. To the north, where the Bonepile Creek started in a ravine in the uplift of the buffalo-grassed hills of our leased section, our growing horse herd was bunched. It occurred to me that if I went south I'd have to borrow horses from Pa. In the range bunch there were two or three partially broken teams, and several saddle horses that I'd ridden enough so that they wouldn't be too salty if I cut them out to use on the trip south. They'd be soft, but would soon harden up on oats and work. I made a wry grimace at the thought, for it caused me to realize how futile and shallow my plans really were. I could get horses from our herd, but in addition I'd need things that cost money—a wagon, tools, harness, possibly haying equipment, grub, and various articles too numerous to mention. I thought of Pa and his everlasting debt and credit that Ma hated so much. I wondered how much Mr. Hardwick, the Coyote Wells banker, would lend a nineteen-year-old kid to undertake a wild goose chase down into the Big Cougar River country.

I rode across the Bonepile Flats, pungent now with the scent of sage, the cactus blooming in glorious splendor, hit the trace again, and headed for town on the lope.

I rode into town and down the street where the businessmen of the town had built their nice homes, just like I had done a year back. Looking back, it seemed much longer than a year, for in that year, in some strange way, I had grown from boy to man. I had seen little of Joan since that day in mid-November when I had just turned the Z Bar O heifers in among our cattle. Then a wild-eyed Joan had galloped up and told me that I must stop calling on her, because if I didn't I would suffer terrible things from a jealous Jed Dupre, backed by his saloonkeeper father, George Dupre. Jed had been going out with Joan before I had taken her to the dance at the Starvation Flats hall, but she had refused to go out with him after that. This had infuriated Jed, particularly since I had beaten him in a fistfight at the hall, after he had called me out and challenged me.

I had laughed at Joan's fears that day, and pulled her from her horse and kissed her. But she had still insisted that my seeing her could only bring me, and perhaps my parents, harm. She had been right, of course, about the harm, because before morning Jed had driven off our twenty blooded heifers, aided by Steve Holden and three other rustlers. This had come within a hair's breadth of costing us not only the heifers but the homestead as well. Shortly after our meeting on the Bonepile Flats the Montana winter had set in, and although I still tried to see Joan our meetings were few and far between and never alone. Her fear for me and mine seemed to have built a barrier between us, preventing us from achieving the warmth and tenderness we'd known. The theft of the heifers, the chase of the rustlers, the meeting, with Pa looking down at Jed and his friends over the barrels of a shotgun, the terrific battle that followed, the capture, the trial, with Jed and Steve being sent to prison for six months in spite of everything George Dupre's high-priced lawyers could do for him, had brought a shadow to Joan's eyes, something that I hesitated to protest or question. During winter and spring's heavy work schedule I'd had little time to protest or question.

Thinking about Joan's standoff attitude, I began to get a little hot under the collar. Maybe she did need to be rammed against the corral fence, like Pa had said. By the time I'd ridden down the alley behind the Preston house and ground hitched Filly, I was in no mood to stall around. Usually I went to the front door and asked Mrs. Preston if I could see Joan in the kitchen. But this time I strode across the yard and knocked on the kitchen door. I heard light footsteps inside and then the door opened and Joan peered out.

"Tom Conway!" she exclaimed. "You shouldn't . . ."

"Shouldn't what?" I demanded, stepping inside, stalking her as she backed away, eyes apprehensive now. "I suppose I should get down and crawl just because I caught Jed Dupre stealing our cattle and had him jailed for six months, in spite of everything his bedamned father could do. Damn it, Joan, us Callahans ain't built that way."

"Callahan!" she exclaimed. "Oh, Tom, you're angry. You never . . ."

"I ain't angry," I declared loudly.

"Yes you are. Your name's Conway, and you never call yourself Callahan unless you're angry. I suppose that now you are going to beat me, like you did Jed Dupre at the dance."

"Damn right," I said, advancing. "Pa said you need ramming against the corral fence and I reckon . . ."

"Ramming . . . corral fence!" she gasped. "Tom Conway, you're crazy."

"Crazy," I rasped at her. "Maybe, but not as crazy as I'm going to be if you don't stop this standoffish business and backin' off just because Jed Dupre or somebody don't like me being around. Now, I'm here to tell you that I don't give a tinker's damn for what Jed Dupre thinks, or his father, or his grandfather, or his great-grandfather, or his great-great-grandfather, or . . ."

She was now backed into the corner between the sink and the wall and could back away no farther.

"And you," I said. "What right have you to lead a person on, and kiss him and such, and then when you get him all riled up back off like you've been doing?"

"Tom Conway," she hissed at me, anger now flaring in her dark eyes. "I did not lead you on. It was your silly teaching me how to shoot at those . . . those dried horse things. You and your making believe that you just wanted to teach me how to shoot. Bears and outlaws about, you said. Even your mother knew that you were just making excuses to take me down to the creek and take advantage of me."

"Take advantage of you!" I gasped. "Why, it was you who turned your head just as I was squinting down your rifle barrel and stuck your lips practically against mine. What was a feller like me supposed to do?"

"Feller like you," she mocked me. "You and your outlaws and bears . . ." And then suddenly her eyes softened and tears appeared at their corners.

"Oh, Tom," she wailed, "what are we fighting about?"

"We're fighting," I said, and all the ire went out of me, and I felt a great wave of tenderness for her come over me, "we're fighting, Joan, because I love you, and because I'm so doggone afraid of losing you that I'm about to die of it."

She put one hand to her mouth, as though in awe, and reached out slowly with the other, her eyes wide and beautiful, with a tear rolling slowly down each cheek.

"Love!" she said. "Tom. Love . . . do you know what that means, what it really means?"

"I know," I said flatly. "It means just the same when I say it as it did when Pa said it to Ma."

"You mean—"

"I mean," I declared, "just what Pa meant, a license and a preacher. . . ."

"Oh, Tom," she gasped. "We can't. Not now. Not right away."

"Not right away," I yelled. "You mean you will if I wait awhile?"

"Of course," she declared. "I really do—I'm not afraid anymore, now that you've said it."

"Said what?"

"Love!" she cried, coming toward me. "That's what you said, Tom Conway. Love. When there is that Jed Dupre, or his father, or his grandfather, or his great-grandfather, or his great-great . . ."

I stopped her lips with mine and found everything was back like it had been before, only a lot better.

"When?" I asked, holding her at arm's length, looking into her eyes.

"Anytime," she cried out, and her laughter tinkled. "Anytime you say, Tom."

Pa had always told me that women were changeable, and now I could see that they were. A minute before, she had told me that we would have to wait awhile, and now she was saying, anytime. As I stood looking at her, a gentle tap came to the door leading from the kitchen and it slowly opened a bit and Mrs. Preston peered in.

"Children," she said brightly, "I couldn't help overhearing. Joan, you may have the rest of the day off. It seems that you may require it. You may use Mr. Preston's horse."

And then she closed the door softly. Joan's face turned red with embarrassment.

"She heard!" she hissed. "We must have talked loud."

"You ninny," I said, reaching for her, "we yelled. Get your bonnet—we're going to ride out to the ranch and tell my folks."

"Oh!" she cried out. "What will they think? Will they like me for a . . . for a daughter-in-law?"

"Like you?" I crowed. "Why do you suppose that Pa told me to ram you against a corral fence?"

"That," she said, "is something I don't understand. I'm going to ask your mother about that."

"I reckon," I said dryly, "that she probably knows. But don't you worry your head about my folks. They've always liked you."

"You're sure?"

"I'm sure. Now let's get that horse saddled and on our way."

When we walked into our house, hand in hand, Pa looked up from reading the Miles City paper. A slow smile came to his eyes.

"Finally corralled you, boy, didn't she," he said. "Knew she would, right from the start."

"Corralled?" Joan queried. "I don't understand."

"It makes no difference," Ma said, coming forward and taking Joan into her arms, "how it happened, just as long as it did happen. We're awfully glad, Joan."

"And I am, too," Pa declared, coming to his feet. "Gad, this makes a man feel like turning handsprings. Never thought I'd see the day."

"What day?" I asked.

"Why," Pa declared, grabbing both Ma and Joan in the wide sweep of his arms, "the day you'd have sense enough to grab off a girl nigh as pretty and fine as your ma. I recall the trouble I had getting her. There was a feller by the name of George Simpson, with waxed mustaches and a squint . . ."

"Never mind George Simpson and his squint," Ma said, breaking free. "It's time for dinner. Let's sit down and eat."

It was while we were eating dinner that the matter of the Cougar River country came up.

"You can't do it," Pa declared. "Takes more than wanting. It takes money for gear, wagon, tools, machinery, supplies, careful planning. You're too young, and it is too far from the railroad for a woman, especially starting on a shoestring. Maybe in a year or so things might work out—you'll be twenty-one."

I was too happy at the moment to argue about it, so I just let Pa ramble on about it, and watched Joan's eyes, questioning my thoughts. After dinner we sat around awhile and then tightened our cinches on the horses and started off for Coyote Wells. On the way we talked.

"You heard," I said, "what Pa said about me wanting to go south to take up government land."

"Yes," she said.

"You realize what that would mean to you, don't you? We'd have nothing to live in but a cabin that we'd have to build ourselves, or fashion from what's left of the old Box Gulch ranch buildings. If we went farther south, say to the Little Cougar River country, it would be even more rugged. If we were able to get started at all, at either place, we'd have to do it on borrowed money."

"I've got over a thousand dollars saved," Joan said.

"Damn it," I declared, "I won't use your money."

"Your wife's money," she teased, and her eyes met mine, velvety and smiling. "Things change between a man and a woman when they get married, Tom. Didn't you know that?"

I rammed Filly against her horse and darn near pulled her from the saddle.

"Stop it," she cried, "and let's make plans. You have been talking about the country down to the south ever since you got back from there. You've got it in your blood, just as sure as your name is Callahan."

She tinkled with laughter.

"Be serious now," I said. "I'm not thinking just of myself and what I want to do. I'm also thinking of Pa and the jam he's in, even if he don't realize it. With the blooded bull I won from Bullow in the horse race, and the top-grade heifers and calves we have from Bullow's herd and the Z Bar O stock, we have the beginnings of a prime outfit. But we now have more stock than we can range, and when the calf crop hits Pa in the face next spring he'll be a cooked goose unless in the meantime I manage to arrange for more graze. Pa's never mentioned it, and I hope that he doesn't get an idea like that in his head, but when I get of age I could file on the Bonepile Flats. Then if we fenced it off, we could keep out other stock, such as Bullow's, and gain a bit. But I wouldn't want to do that to Bill Bullow, nor would I want to use my precious filing right on an alkali flat that's not fit to live on."

"And," Joan said, "you think that you could do better down south?"

"Better!" I crowed. "Why, down there you can file on six hundred forty acres under the Grazing Land Act, while here you can only file on three hundred twenty acres under the homestead laws. I know of places down there where I could build a cabin overlooking a running stream, with shade trees overhead, with water to irrigate a truck garden, and what's more, with thousands of acres of open range around it. Here, we try to find enough range for a hundred head.

Down there the problem would be to find enough cattle to cover the range. I could—"

"You could," Joan interrupted. "But can we? Can we, Tom, or are you just dreaming, as I was before you asked me to marry you, that you'd someday come and ask me?"

"You were!" I cried out. "You were actually waiting for me to come and ask you, while I was dragging around . . . well, I'll be damned."

"Yes," she said. "And now that you have asked me, I want you to forget all about me living in a cabin that we had to build ourselves fifty miles from the railroad. If you marry me, Tom, I'm going to be your wife, really your wife, if you go fifty miles or five hundred miles, whether we live in a shanty or a palace. I want you to really understand that."

"I understand," I said. "I understand that in some wonderful way that I don't yet understand, I've got me a woman like my mother."

"That don't make much sense," Joan laughed, "but I'll take it as the compliment it was intended to be. Your mother is a swell person."

"You say that it's a dream, Joan," I said, "and maybe it is. But all we need to make it come true is enough money to get started. I'll make up a list of what we'll need, and find out how much it will cost. Then I'll talk to the banker, Hardwick, and get in touch with the land office and get survey maps. I'll have a million things to do."

"Among other things you've got to do," Joan teased, "is a little thing like, we'll say, getting married."

"Gosh, Joan," I burst out, "a man can't marry a girl until he has someplace to take her to after he marries her."

"You mean," Joan cried out, her dark eyes hard to read, "that you intend to go south and build your cabin and everything, which may take months, before we get married?"

I suddenly found myself facing a question that I couldn't

answer. We talked about it and chewed it back and forth all the way into Prestons' place. On the way we stopped off at the post office and found a telegram there which said that Uncle Pete would arrive on the train in the morning.

"I've got to get this news right out to the ranch," I told Joan. "Ma will want some time to get things ready for Uncle Pete's arrival."

I unsaddled Preston's horse, rubbed it down and stabled it, kissed Joan as thoroughly as I knew how, and headed for the ranch on the lope, without the slightest idea that Uncle Pete's arrival was going to change things entirely about going south to take up land.

CHAPTER THREE

When I hit the ranch with the news, Ma started rushing around doing the things women do when they expect company. But Pa was calm.

"Heck," he complained, "you don't need to make ary fuss over Pete. Now if we just had a jug of hard cider we could bed him down in the barn and the old coot would feel right at home."

"Old?" I asked. "How old is Uncle Pete?"

"About your father's age," Ma said. "Maybe forty-two or -three. You must remember, Tom, that your pa and Uncle Pete were kids together and that they are sort of friendly enemies. Think the world of each other but wouldn't admit it if it killed them. Always wrangling. If one said the sky was blue the other'd swear it was green, or pink, or purple."

"Fishin' chickens off the barn," Pa mumbled.

"What's that?" Ma asked.

"Never mind," Pa said. "Maybe the old coot has changed some. Should be old enough now to have some sense—still, he didn't have any the last time I saw him, and that was only six, seven years back. And, Tom, don't you go to prodding him about that Cougar River country. Get him more'n a mile or two from town and he'd be completely bewildered. Chances are he can find some land close by to file on, maybe the Bonepile. It's got graze and water."

"Graze and water," I scoffed. "Potholes that nigh dry up in summer, and bog cattle down when they try to drink. Graze that's only good in spring and early summer. Alkali where you couldn't raise even a truck garden."

"Anyway," Pa declared, "you won't find a back-Easter like Pete wanting to dash off into the wilderness. Back-Easters are mighty cautious."

"You," Ma said, "were a back-Easter yourself."

"No," Pa said, "I didn't go East until I was six or seven years old. I was born in Minnesota. That's why I don't talk with the broad *a* the New Englanders use. And you'll notice when I filed on land I got it close to town. You just forget mentioning the Cougar River country to Pete, Tom."

"But don't you forget, Pa," I said determinedly, "that we now have over a hundred head of cattle and a horse herd and not enough land to graze them on, let alone winter feed them, that is, unless you plan to cut your grain crop for hay like you did last year. We've simply got to have more land, or get rid of our blooded breeding heifers. If we have to do that we'll be right back where we started from, borrowing money to stay afloat, mortgaging the homestead again."

Pa gave me a long, calculating, disgusted look.

"Now that you've got it all added up," he said sarcastically, "maybe you can go ahead and figure it out, too. Me, I'm going to bed. That train gets in early in the morning."

Since Uncle Pete was riding the fast Milwaukee railroad train, the Olympian, which got into Coyote Wells at bare dawn, we had to get up before daylight and get under way for town. When the train pulled in a lone figure got off and stood swiveling his head around, looking the country over. When I walked up to him and he turned around he looked just about as I had remembered him, a small man with a reddish, walrus mustache flowing beneath a long nose and florid face. His head was rather narrow and his neck appeared a bit overlong, with a prominent, bobbing Adam's apple. His eyebrows, like his mustache, were exceedingly heavy and bushy, and one seemed to be placed higher than the other, giving him a sort of quizzical look. This, with his dark, expressive brown eyes, gave him an appearance of perpetual astonishment. There was a slight touch of the

Welsh in his tongue and he sometimes used the broad *a* of
New England, especially when he became overly excited. In
spite of my changed appearance, he knew me at once. His
grip was astonishingly strong when he grasped my hand, as
is the grip, I found, of most any man who has spent years
milking cows.

"Baah Jove," he exclaimed heartily, "if it ain't little Tom-
mie grown up. Man, am I glad to get off that bloody train.
First few miles on that gallopin' goose ain't so bad, but after
three or four days of it a person's bones begin to hang and
rattle. Ah, here comes John and Trix."

Pa fetched him such a clatter on the back I thought his
teeth would fly out. Ma put her arms around him and I
could see that she thought a lot of her sister's husband. Pete
stepped back after the greetings were over and peered about
at the prairie stretching endlessly in all directions, a rolling
sea of sage and grass, broken only by homestead barbed-
wire fencing here and there.

"Why didn't you folks tell me," he said, "that you lived
on a bloody desert? Ain't a tree in sight and I'll swear that I
can see for fifty miles."

"That's why we like it," Pa said.

"You suah, John?" Uncle Pete inquired, a look of humor
now in his eyes. "You suah you like it, or are you just plain
stuck with it?"

Uncle Pete slapped his knees and cackled with glee.

"Stuck with it," he burbled, "and too damned stiff-necked
to admit it. Well, John, you always was a mite peculiar."

"Peculiar!" Pa echoed. "Did you say that I was . . ."

Hastily Ma slipped her arm through Uncle Pete's and
swung him around.

"Let's get Uncle Pete's luggage," she said, "and head for
home. I felt a little lost in this big country myself, Pete,
when I first came, but you'll get used to it."

All the way to the ranch we kept pointing out things of
interest to Uncle Pete, such as jackrabbits jumping up now

and then and flocks of sage hens walking across the trace, the distant prairie dogs barking on the old, abandoned Bill Turner place. We pointed out Pilot Butte, upthrusting from the prairie to the northwest, and Antelope Butte to the southeast. I noticed that Uncle Pete peered down into the muddy water of Bonepile Creek as we drove over the narrow bridge.

"Any fish in there, Tom?" he asked.

"Some little sucker fingerlings," I said. "Not more than two or three inches long."

"Tried her out then, I see." He chuckled. "Thought you would."

"Yeah," I said, "but we sure pulled some big catfish out of the Box Gulch Creek when . . ."

I caught Pa's frown and shut up, but Uncle Pete was already solidly hooked.

"You don't say, Tom. Now do you suppose that we could get up early in the morning and hook up the buggy? Or maybe we could walk it? How far is this creek?"

"We ain't got no buggy," Pa said. "And besides, you ain't got ary idea of what this country is like, Pete. That crick is three days' ride to the south, through a country full of all sorts of dangers, rattlesnakes, outlaws, and such."

"Outlaws?" Uncle Pete queried.

"Bet your life," Pa declared. "Only last fall five of them stole some of our cattle. Me and the boy here and Shagnasty Smith had to trail them down. I had a double-barreled shotgun. . . ."

"I got one of those," Uncle Pete said brightly, "in my luggage. Then, because I figured that I was coming out to wild country, I bought me a government surplus rifle. Six feet long, the thing is, with a bore you can stick your finger down. Man don't hardly need to hit anything with that gun. The racket it makes is enough to knock the feathers off'n a goose at a hundred paces. Practiced firing it in my pasture and the sheriff came out from North Wilberham to inquire what the hell was goin' on. And then, old man Worrel—you know him, John, short, fat feller owns the farm joining mine. Always peering down holes. Well, he got a sprained neck."

"Sprained neck?" Pa inquired.

"Yeah, you know how he was always getting down on his hands and knees and peering down varmint holes. He'd gather some hair off the sides of the holes so he could calculate what kind of a varmint was using the hole—fox, woodchuck, or skunk. Then he'd set his traps accordingly. You know, foxes are awfully smart, but woodchucks and skunks are trapped easy."

"I know," Pa said, "but what's this got to do with old man Worrel getting a sprained neck?"

"Well, it appears that Worrel was down on his hands and knees, peering down a woodchuck hole, when I let go with this 45–70 rifle of mine. Right startling noise, if I do say so. Worrel, he tried to get the hell out of there without first pullin' his head out'n the hole. He was pretty mad about it. Said he was damned glad that I was selling out and leaving the country."

"I wouldn't be surprised," Pa said dryly.

"This rifle of mine," Uncle Pete went on, "was just like brand new, out of the Springfield armory. Got a bayonet with it, too."

"What the deuce would you want a bayonet for?" Pa asked.

"Haven't the slightest idea," Pete said. "Yet. But I'll think of something."

Pa shuddered.

"And," Uncle Pete added, "I've brought along my fishing tackle."

"I'll bet you did," Pa said. "Caught any chickens off your barn roof lately?"

"Harrumph!" Pete cleared his throat as he apparently

thought that one out, and then said, dryly, "You recall that, do you, John?"

"I recall it, and also the pigs and the bacon rind."

Pete chuckled deep in his throat.

"What kids won't do," he said.

"What on earth," Ma asked, "are you two talking about?"

"Nothing in particular," Pa replied, waving his arm at just about the sorriest-appearing piece of real estate in Montana, the Bonepile Creek Flats, white in places with alkali deposits. "Now there is as likely a piece of homestead ground as you are apt to see. And you're lucky that it's still open for filing."

Uncle Pete peered at the land in astonishment.

"If that," he said, "is the best I'm apt to see around here, I'd better head out back East fast. That land ain't fit to raise mice on. And what's that white stuff scattered around on it?"

"Alkali," I said, and just to egg Pa on, added, "and there isn't any of that along Box Gulch Creek down south. But there sure are a lot of trees."

"Trees! You don't say. Any of them apple trees?"

"Apple trees," Pa snorted in disgust. "There ain't none, and if there were any the cougars would have eaten all the apples. That's cougar country down there."

"Cats," Uncle Pete said, "don't eat apples." And then he gave me a long, slow look and winked at me.

"John," he said, "I kind of get the idea that you don't want me to get a yen to go down south and that Tom here does."

He chuckled, and right then I realized that my uncle Pete was a whole lot smarter than Pa had led me to believe.

"Well," Pa said, "I might as well own up to it, Pete. Tom here, being only nineteen and not yet dry behind the ears, has been hankering for that country to the south ever since we drove a herd through it last fall. But older folks, like you and me, know more about which side of the bed to get out of on a cold morning."

"Maybe so," Pete said, and then, "How big were those catfish you caught out of that brook?"

"Crick," Pa said, "not brook. They weren't very big. I heaved them out like they was minnows."

"Yes," I said perversely, "and the three of us ate on them for three days. Had some left when we got down on the Big Cougar."

"Three days!" Pete exclaimed. "They must have been whoppers."

After we got home and had dinner we sat around and talked and Uncle Pete told us what he really had in mind.

"All these years," he explained, "I've been stuck on a forty-acre farm, putting up hay and milking cows. From Trix's letters I got the idea that everyone out here has hundreds of acres. So, seeing that me and Ina always have been frugal—"

"Stingy," Pa cut in.

"Frugal," Pete said firmly. "And I got a good price for my farm, to boot. So I've got enough laid away to get some land out here and start over. Sort of get out and stretch my legs."

"Stretch your legs out here," Pa said, "and you're apt to walk off into the distance and never show up again."

"Now, John," Ma said, "you stop trying to frighten Pete."

"Frighten!" Uncle Pete perked up like an insulted banty rooster. "Never been frightened in my bloody life. Scared, yes. Frightened, no."

"What's the difference?" I asked.

"Don't know. Since I have only experienced the one, and not the other, I ain't able to exactly tell."

Pa looked disgusted.

"Anyway," Uncle Pete went on, "I've got enough money laid away, I reckon, to grab off one of these government homesteads. What do you raise out here, John? That looks like wheat out there."

"Oats," Pa said, even though it was actually wheat. "And don't you worry about it. We'll be able to locate you on a three-hundred-twenty-acre homestead around here someplace. Of course it won't be as good as this one, but you'll be able to farm all you want. Milk cows, for that matter, if you can find any around here that a person would be able to ketch."

Pa chuckled.

I didn't get a chance to really talk to Uncle Pete until we went to bed. Since we only had two bedrooms, he and I slept together. And no matter what Pa claims, it was Uncle Pete, not me, who brought up the matter of the Cougar River country.

"What's this," he asked, "that's going on here between you and John? Every time you mention this country to the south he begins to knock it. Why don't he want me to go down there?"

"Because," I told him, "he knows that if you do I'll probably go with you. I'd planned to go anyway, as soon as I can rake up the money for an outfit."

"Why are you so set on going?"

"Because," I told him, "we've now got over a hundred head of horses and cattle on the range, and that is more than our range will handle. As it is, they are apt to go into the winter poor, unless Pa cuts some of his grain crop for hay and starts feeding early. By the time the calves come off next spring we'll be in a real squeeze. Down south, a person can take up a whole section, six hundred forty acres, under the Grazing Act, while here you can only take up three hundred twenty acres, under the homestead laws. I'm too young yet to file, but I could squat on land and maybe hold it until filing age. Anyway, I've got to get more range or we'll be right back where we were before we got the blooded breeding stock that we have now. We've gone as far as we can here. We've got to expand or sit still."

"And," Uncle Pete said dryly, "you're too young and hot-blooded to sit still. Glad you told me about it. We'll talk about it some more in the morning. If it's money for an outfit you need, you can forget it. I've got the money."

"I'd never think," I declared, "of using your money."

"Of course not," Uncle Pete said. "As John told you, I'm stingy. But if I decide to go down there I'll need a guide and a hired hand. What are the going wages around here?"

"Thirty and found," I said, and felt like raring out of bed and dancing a jig. It looked to me now as though I just might get down into that country where trees grew and water ran and timber wolves still howled, the kind of country that Shagnasty Smith liked. I was going to talk some more about it but Uncle Pete was snoring.

We talked about it plenty in the morning. And for a week Pa drove Pete around the country, and down to the land office, trying to locate a homestead for him. But everything worthwhile had been filed on, and either had a settler on it or had been patented and sold to somebody big enough to buy and handle it. We found a couple or three homesteads open in the badlands, but Pete wouldn't have anything to do with them.

"Bloody land," he complained, "stands on end. Looks like the place I reckon I'll go to when I die, and I don't plan to press the matter."

During this time I had stopped working on Uncle Pete. He was no more afraid of going fifty miles from a railroad than a bee was afraid of honey—that is, if there was a fishing stream about. But I had to keep working on Pa, warning him about our shortage of range, about the increase we'd get with the spring calf crop. This had been my deliberate strategy from the start, to build up our herd until it got so big that Pa would be forced to expand. And now this point was reached and I actually had Pa over a barrel, so to speak. I wondered if I should have a guilty conscience about it. If it worked out for the best I'd feel proud and strut a bit, but if it didn't work out—well, Pa would still have his well-bred stock to sell to pay his debts and be no worse off than if I hadn't tried. With this thought my conscience had to be satisfied.

"This is the way I see it, John," Uncle Pete said at the end of the week. "Tom's right. You need more graze and there's nothing around here that I'd want to file on or buy in on."

"Well," Pa said, "I guess there's no harm in going down and taking a look at it. But I'm warning you, Pete, you won't like it. It's too far from the railroad and supplies."

"How would we go about seeing it?"

"Well," I said, "there's two ways. We can take a couple saddle horses and a pack horse and ride down and back—take us maybe six days or so. Or we can load up a wagon with everything you'd need to build a cabin and settle."

"That last would be foolish," Pa said. "You want to look first. Not lookin' first is like grabbing a cat in a gunny sack."

It was along toward evening then, so I told Pa I'd ride into town, and of course Pa knew where I was going, and told Pete.

"The boy's got a girl in town," he told Pete, "and that's why he's so all-fired anxious to strike out for himself down south. Wants to get a place of his own to take his bride to."

"You don't say."

"I do say," Pa said. "Thought you'd be interested."

When I rode into Coyote Wells the first persons I saw were Jed Dupre and Steve Holden. I hadn't seen either of them since I had testified at the trial that had sent them to prison for six months. The three rustlers with them, Henry Hutton, Jim Brokaw, and Ben Jacob, had been given one-year sentences, but George Dupre's high-priced lawyers had gotten Jed and his pal Steve off with lesser sentences.

As Jed and Steve rode down the main street of Coyote

Wells toward me I couldn't see that prison had changed
them any. Jed was riding his beautiful, long-legged black,
sitting cockily in his black silver-mounted saddle, dressed in
black shirt, black chaps, and black hat and gloves to match.
Steve, as always, was his shadow, riding bold-eyed beside
him. The pair of them deliberately blocked my path and
pulled up. Jed's dark eyes bored into mine, filled with
hatred.

"Conway," he gritted out, "we're going to make you pay
for every day we spent in that lousy jail, one way or another. You just wait and see."

"Why don't you come off it, Jed," I said, "and call it
quits. You got caught rustling our cattle and paid for it. If
you're smart you'll let that be the end of it."

"I'll see you in hell first, Conway. And if you're smart
you'll stay away from Joan Bauer now that I'm back. No
damned shack-crawling honyoker is going to steal my girl."

I just sat there on Filly, looking at him, wondering how
he could possibly think so crooked, believe what was not
true.

"If you think that she's your girl, Jed," I said flatly, "you
are an even bigger fool than I thought you were. Now get
out of my way."

I touched Filly lightly with the spurs and rode right at the
pair. At first I thought they were going to try to stop me,
but then they swerved aside to let me ride between them.
Out of the corners of my eyes I saw Sheriff Matt Fillbuster
standing on the boardwalk, watching us. I wondered what
the two would have done if he hadn't been there. I wondered what they might try to do if I should meet them down
on the Box Gulch country and if they knew that I was planning on taking up land down there. Joan Bauer answered
that question as soon as she had answered my knock on the
kitchen door and I had freed her lips long enough for her to
talk.

"Jed and Steve are back," she said, her eyes worried,

"and they know that you are planning to take up land down south."

"How do you know that?" I asked.

"Women," she said, "have a way of knowing things in a small town like this. Jed has told around that he and Steve plan on going down south to look the land over. I'll bet that they are doing it just to spite you."

"Why me?" I asked. "Pa and Shagnasty Smith, and Matt Fillbuster and a judge and jury were all in on sending them to jail."

"I don't know why they should pick on you, Tom, but . . ."

"I know," I told her. "Jed is like his father. He can't bear to let anybody else have anything that he wants. He can't bear to have anything he wants taken away from him, just like you told me last November when you met me on the Bonepile Flats, just before Jed and his bunch drove off our cattle. The fellow's looney. He actually had the nerve to tell me to stay away from you, that you were his girl. Well, don't worry your pretty head about it. Jed and Steve have awfully big mouths."

I told her not to worry but I was plenty worried. If Jed and Steve did take a ride down south, they would naturally follow the same trace that we did when we went with the wagon. They were bound to see the old Box Gulch ranch buildings and might suspect that this was the land I wanted. Both of them were old enough to file on land. But I was pretty sure that neither Jed nor Steve would want to live on the land, as the law required. This would mean that George Dupre would arrange for one of his men to do the filing. On one or more of his ranch holdings he had plenty of riders who might do the deed, for a price. I had made up my mind by now that the site of the old Box Gulch buildings was the land I wanted—at least I didn't want Dupre to add it to his already extensive holdings. I headed out for the ranch at the lope as soon as I could without frightening Joan about it.

CHAPTER FOUR

It took quite a bit of explaining to Uncle Pete to make him understand the situation that existed between us and Jed Dupre and Steve Holden, and make him understand that these men were really dangerous.

"You mean to tell me," he said incredulously, "that you actually had a gun battle with these bloody characters and sent them up to the bleeding jail, and that now they are out again and liable to interfere with my taking up land down south?"

Uncle Pete glared around with his Adam's apple popping up and down and his red mustache bristling with indignation.

"Why," he declared, "I never even seen these hooligans. Baah Jove, it seems to be dangerous to even know you and Tom here."

"Is that so," Pa said. "Well, you're lucky to have us around. You wouldn't last half a second with desperadoes like this pair."

"Is that so," Pete said. "Well, let me tell you something—"

"This isn't getting us anywhere," I cut in.

"What are we going to do about it?" Uncle Pete asked.

"Forget about going," Pa said.

"No!" Uncle Pete said explosively. "Nobody is going to make Pete L. Evans tuck his tail between his legs."

"The L," Pa said dryly, "stands for Lunkhead."

"Louie," Uncle Pete said. "If I only knew more about the country down there. Tom, you tell me what should be done."

"Well," I said, "I saw a lot of that country down there along the Box Gulch and the Little and Big Cougar rivers, and I made a lot of plans about going down on the Little Cougar and taking up land. I had a lot of wild ideas. But when it comes right down to it, I know that the best thing to do is to get the best land that you can as near to supplies and market as you can. We'll have to drive some of our stock down there and we'll have to drive some back again to ship out to Chicago or Kansas City. The very best location I saw down there was the site where the old buildings of the old Box Gulch ranch stand. That's about fifty miles from the railroad and Coyote Wells. I checked with the land office and this section has been surveyed and is open for filing. Jed Dupre and Steve are bound to see the place if they go down—but maybe they are just talking. But we'd better get on down there and look at that land, Uncle Pete, to see if you want to file on it."

"You are too young to file, Tom," Pete said. "I'd be filing on land that you want."

"Yes," I said, "but I'd a lot rather you had it than to see George Dupre have one of his hands, or maybe Jed or Steve, file on it. If you had it I could file on some connecting land along the creek and we could be neighbors. If the Dupres were in there I wouldn't be able to get by around them by myself."

"You see, Pete," Pa explained, "men like George Dupre —he's a wealthy saloonkeeper, and well-to-do, big ranchers often have their hired hands file on government land with an agreement that when they prove up on it and get title to it, they will turn it over to them for a set figure. Often they furnish grub and such while their hired hand is living on the place long enough to get title. It is against the law to do this, but it goes on all the time. It is hard to prove that there was any agreement, that the fellow didn't just decide to sell. Dupre would back his son, or even his saloon swamper, to do this if Jed asked him to and he thought that the land would be worth the effort or what he put into it. He might even do it for spite, because he certainly didn't like us ketching Jed rustling and appearing against him at the trial. But what of it? You wouldn't like it down there anyway, Pete. Let it go."

"There ain't any harm in looking it over," Pete said. "I just might find it to be just what I'd want."

No harm in looking it over, I thought. Looking over a stream running placidly through a sea of virgin grass, where the meadowlarks sang during the days and the lobo wolves still howled at night. I knew how that place had appeared to me; I wondered how it would appear to Uncle Pete. Did life in Massachusetts, putting up hay and milking cows, with a trolley car into town, fit a man to get the feel of such a place? It depends, I thought, on what a man has in his heart, what reaches out to touch him where he lives. Me, I could see, in my mind's eye; our cattle roaming in lush bunch grass, wandering down to drink from the stream, while we looked out the window of our cabin, Joan and I, in the shade of the box elder trees. It was my dream, but if Uncle Pete had to file on it to keep the dream in the family, that's the way it would have to be.

"Well," Uncle Pete said, rising and dusting his hands together. "How do we get started on this expedition?"

"How good can you ride a horse?" I asked.

"Been riding them all my life."

"Yeah," Pa chuckled, "a plow horse, from the field to the barn, sitting on the harness, hanging on to the hames. Never set a saddle in your life."

"What difference does it make? Saddle or harness—it's all the same."

"You don't say," Pa said, his blue eyes taking on that innocent look he always gets in them when he has deviltry up his sleeve. "Just the same, Tom, I think you'd best make sure he gets a real gentle horse to ride. Maybe that stocky bay, Chub, would be about right."

Chub was a proud cut gelding, a good enough saddle horse except for the fact that he liked to take a few bucking jumps every morning. He'd thrown me a couple of times when I got careless.

"No," I said, "I'll ride Filly and Uncle Pete can ride Segundo. I imagine that Shagnasty will want to ride Big Red or Two Step."

"Segundo," Pa echoed. "If anybody rides Segundo it will be me. And what do you want Shagnasty Smith along for? Is this a look-see trip or an invasion?"

"You can't go, Pa," I said. "Who'll take care of the place?"

"Ma can milk the one cow, feed the chickens, and slop the hogs. The water's not low yet in the Bonepile so there won't be any mud-bogged cattle. Besides, Mike Flaherty will come over and look after things for the few days we'll be gone. Dang right I'm going. I want to see what kind of land you two have in mind to range my cattle on later on. But what in the world will we need Shagnasty for on this trip?"

"We needed him pretty badly, Pa," I said, "the last time we met Jed Dupre and Steve Holden. We just might meet them again on this trip."

Pa got a startled look in his eyes as the possibility struck him.

"Yeah," he said. "I see. Pete, did you say that you had a double-barreled shotgun in your luggage?"

"Sure have," Pete said, "and I also got my fishin' tackle."

Pa groaned.

"This ain't going to be a land-hunting party," he declared. "It's going to be a fishing trip, sure as shooting."

"When can we start?" Uncle Pete asked enthusiastically.

"The sooner the better," I said. "I'll ride over to Bill Bullow's and see if he will let us have Shagnasty for a week. On my way back I'll run Lady Bird in for Uncle Pete to ride. I'm sure that if we can get Shagnasty he'll be able to bring along a couple pack horses to carry our camp gear. Since you are going along, Pa, why don't you and Pete run into Coyote Wells and get what grub we'll need. A week's supply should do it. We can live off the country a lot. There are young sage hens around now, and there will be rabbits in the coulees—cottontails. Pete will need some different clothes, riding boots, chaps, and so forth. Maybe Rose Shagnasty will come over with Shagnasty and stay with Ma, like she did the last time."

"This," declared Uncle Pete, "is going to be more fun than the time when Ina poured my hard cider in the watering trough."

"How's that?" Pa asked. "Cider in the watering trough?"

"I'll tell you about that later," Uncle Pete said. "Let's get into town and buy those cowboy clothes I'm going to need."

Uncle Pete thought the trip was going to be fun, and it well might be. But if Jed and Steve were down there at the same time that we were, it might be far different fun than Uncle Pete had ever encountered back in Massachusetts.

Once we had made up our minds to go, things moved along pretty fast. But not fast enough to suit me. Mike and Dennis Flaherty and Grandma and Grandpa Hobson came calling, anxious to see and meet Uncle Pete. The news that we were going south to look for land spread like a prairie fire, but I did everything I could to give the impression that we didn't have any particular land singled out for attention. Bill Bullow was glad to lend us Shagnasty and a couple of pack horses.

"You're doing the right thing," Bill told me. "We've got so many head stacked up on the Bonepile range now that even if I pulled all my stuff off of there you'd still overgraze it. Your Pa's going to have to cut an awful lot of hay, or buy it, to put what he's got through the winter strong enough to calve well come spring. But if you could get settled down south in time to drive a good share of your herd down there, they'd winter fat as butter in those sheltered coulees. That bunch grass down there can't be beat."

"Why then," I asked, "did the old-timers lose so much in 1887?"

"Because," Bullow said, "they tried to run too many with too little help. They didn't put up feed, and they hit two or three hard winters in a row. A man who's on his toes, uses his head down there, and profits by past mistakes can make a good thing of it in the Box Gulch country. I'm damned glad that you are taking Shagnasty along, especially since you tell me that Jed Dupre and Steve Holden may be down there. That pair hates your guts, Tom. They'll bear watching."

The meeting between Shagnasty Smith and Uncle Pete was something to see. Shagnasty stood nigh seven feet tall, with the shoulders of a wrestler, his great, shaggy head, his expressive brown eyes peering out from a wreath of reddish-brown hair and whiskers, his hat hanging down the back of his neck on a leather thong, his Indian blood giving him a hawkish look. He towered over Uncle Pete, who had just tried on his new cowboy clothing. Pete stood there, looking up at Shagnasty in astonishment, dressed in a pair of pinkish woolly chaps, new silk-stitched Justin riding boots with long-shanked, star-roweled spurs, his thin features shaded by a new Stetson which was too large for him and came down to his ears. There was just one thing in common with this pair, and it seemed to form a bond between them. This was the rifle they each carried: a long-barreled, government-surplus, swinging-block, single-shot 45–70, with a ramrod under the barrel. Uncle Pete was just showing the rifle to Pa when Shagnasty arrived and was introduced.

"By Gar!" Shagnasty declared. "This little feller carries big gun, just like Shagnasty."

The big man wrenched his old and rusted weapon from the saddle and showed it to Uncle Pete, and instantly they were friends. Uncle Pete took an instant liking to Shagnasty and followed him around like a dog, always at his heels as he helped prepare to leave. Later Shagnasty told me, "Little man my friend. Damn big liar. Good. You bet."

Perhaps Shagnasty was recalling his youth, when the biggest Indian chiefs were usually the bucks who could tell the biggest whoppers around the campfire. Shagnasty never tired of hearing Uncle Pete's windy tales, and he particularly liked the one about his neighbor who became so startled by the boom of Uncle Pete's 45–70 that he tried to run with his head still down a woodchuck hole.

"Old man Worrel," Shagnasty would chuckle, "big damn fool. Nobody run with head in hole. Break neck."

One of Uncle Pete's biggest stories was about how he'd stopped making apple cider.

"Ina got mad one day," Uncle Pete explained, "and rolled my cider keg out'n the cellar and dumped it in the watering trough, the pigs' trough, the chickens' drinking pan. She figured that if I saw the effect my hard cider had on the animals maybe I'd quit drinking it myself."

"What effect did it have?" I asked.

"The place," Pete said, "was a bedlam. The cows was mooing and staggering around and one of them toppled into the pigpen, breaking down the fence. The pigs got out and went skahooting around the yard, squealing like old Harry himself. My horse galloped around and around in the pasture, neighing until he fell down. The chickens all went spraddle-legged. Our banty rooster whipped the tar out'n a gander because the goose was so loaded he couldn't locate the little feller. Our roosters started fighting, and every time one of them fell down, the other one thought he'd won the battle and started crowing and flapping his wings. This made the other one mad and he got up and they started the whole deal over again. Seems like after that I never did get to fill that keg up again. Just the same, I'd like to have a gallon or so of good, hard cider along on this trip. Good for what ails a man."

We had considerable difficulty in getting Uncle Pete up on his horse in any sort of riding shape. He hung on to the saddlehorn at first with both hands, accidentally jabbed his spurs into Lady Bird's ribs, and got rolled off backward when she responded. We made him take the spurs off, shortened up his stirrups, shut our ears to his complaints, and got on with the business of getting started.

We finally got strung out from Coyote Wells in early June, with four saddle horses and two pack horses. I was riding Filly, and Pa was on Segundo. Since Shagnasty was an expert with packs and the diamond hitch for our pack horses, we were a pretty well-organized group. Bullow had lent Uncle Pete a saddle with a rifle scabbard, but Shagnasty had to cut the end off of the scabbard, just like he had done with his own, to permit the long barrels of their 45–70s to thrust through. I carried my 30–30 and had the little .22 single-shot rifle on one of the pack horses, to be used for small game for the fry pan. The pack horses carried bedrolls, canvas tarps, grub, cooking gear, ax, and so forth. We figured that we'd make better time going down to the Box Gulch on the horses than we had the previous fall with the wagon. On that trip we'd made it to Elk Creek the first night and hit the Box Gulch the second night out. We'd made long days of it, traveling until dark. Now, with saddle horses, we thought that we could hit the Elk Creek camp in daylight and do the same with our Box Gulch arrival.

"Remember," Pa said as we started up the long grade out of Coyote Wells toward the rim of the hills beyond, "that it isn't as far to the old Box Gulch building site as it is to where we made camp that night on the creek."

I was riding Filly, Pa was on Segundo, and Shagnasty rode Big Red and led the pack horses, which, he claimed, would follow unled after we got a ways from town. The evening before we started, I had ridden into town to see Joan and ask her about the latest town gossip.

"I haven't seen either Jed or Steve," she told me, "and without coming right out and asking about them I haven't been able to find out where they are. They could have ridden south or they could be hanging around Jed's father's saloon, playing poker and drinking."

"Or," I said, "out on one of George Dupre's various spreads. You'd think that he'd put Jed to work now that he's back again and make him earn his salt. Anyway, don't worry about them."

"Oh, Tom," she cried out, "I wish that you weren't going way off down there where anything could happen to you."

"Nothing bad is going to happen," I comforted her, "and my going is what is going to bring about everything we want in the future. I'm going to make us a home down there, Joan, and then I'm going to marry you and take you to it."

Now, riding Filly up the long rise out of Coyote Wells, I could still feel the warmth of her lips on mine as I left her, and the promise in her eyes remained with me, bringing a feeling of strength to my shoulders.

When we finally topped the rise, passed over it, so that Coyote Wells was lost to view behind us, I got that same feeling of pleasure and exhilaration that I had experienced on the other trip. But now the landscape had changed. Then there had been the brownness of fall, the dusty appearance of the sage, the lack of the songs of the meadowlarks, which had largely gone south. Now the great land flowed away from us, still holding the greening of spring, and meadowlarks sprang up before us, trilling their melodious song. The thought that before us lay a hundred miles of wilderness, down to the Big Cougar River, gave a man a feeling of wanting to press on, on to lose himself in that great vastness of prairie and coulee and gulch and ravine. Looking back, I could see Shagnasty's shaggy head towering over

Uncle Pete's, and the bobbing backs of the heavily laden pack horses. Thinking about what lay at the end of our trail brought me a temporary feeling of sadness, for Uncle Pete would file on the old Box Gulch headquarters and it would be lost to me. But I also had the sure feeling that we must grab it now or lose it to George Dupre, in one way or another that he might devise. We rode on into the unending sea of sage and grass, toward whatever might lie ahead.

CHAPTER FIVE

As we strung out south, alternating between walking and trotting the horses, Uncle Pete got by all right at the walk but did a lot of bouncing in his saddle on the trot. With every bounce his too-large Stetson hat sank lower and lower over his ears until only his long nose and his flowing mustache could be seen.

"Must have a rubber bottom," Pa declared. "Bounces like a rubber ball."

"Balderdash!" Uncle Pete came back at him. "You blighters fixed me up with the roughest riding horse in Montana. I figured that you were up to something like that when I saw you snickering together before we started."

"Lady Bird," I said, "has an easy gait, Uncle Pete."

"Him learn pretty quick," Shagnasty commented.

We made much better time with the saddlers than we had with the wagon on the other trip. When Pa broke out his watch and called for a halt at noon we were well past the place where we had nooned before. Uncle Pete practically rolled off his horse and lay flat on the ground.

"I ain't going a foot farther," he proclaimed, "on that hump-backed camel you call a horse. How far have we come, anyway?"

"We called it eighteen miles to our noon camp last year," I said, "and we are well past that place, so we've come over twenty miles from the ranch, and over fifteen from Coyote Wells. That's a long ride for a man who is not used to the saddle, Uncle Pete."

"The old coot'll never make it," Pa said.

"Who says I won't?" Pete sat up in indignation. "I never saw an Irisher who could outdo a Welshman at anything. When you arrive at wherever it is we're headed for, I'll be right there too."

"Eat, not talk," Shagnasty said, moving to the pack horses to break out the food Ma had put up for our first meals—fried chicken, bread, buffalo berry jam, and a flask of cold tea. As he spread the food out on a canvas tarp laid on the ground, I moved to loosen cinches and grain the horses.

"Wish we could water them," I said, "but they'll have to wait until we hit the Elk tonight, unless we run into a buffalo wallow holding water yet."

"It'll be pitch dark by the time we hit the Elk," Pa remarked, "just like it was last fall."

"No," Shagnasty said, waving a huge fist, wrapped around a sandwich, at the sun. "This be June, not October."

"That's right," I said. "It don't get dark nearly as quick now as it did in October. We should be able to make camp on the Elk in daylight."

After we had eaten and rested a few minutes we started out again, sometimes riding bunched when the terrain permitted it and at other times strung out in single file. It was a beautiful June day, the prairie drowsing in a warm sun, and then suddenly, like things are apt to do in Montana, the whole deal blew apart. A rattlesnake slithered out from the sage and coiled by Lady Bird's feet and sent out its deadly, buzzing warning. Lady Bird shied aside so violently that Uncle Pete toppled from the saddle, and sprawled within striking distance of the coiled reptile. When the snake rattled I was riding just in front of Uncle Pete and Shagnasty was riding just behind him. Filly heard the sound and leaped ahead, but I came down hard on her neck with the reins and jabbed her with the off spur, swinging her around just in time to see Shagnasty go into the most fluid, beautiful action that I had ever witnessed. He flipped the long-barreled 45–70 from its scabbard, heeled back the huge hammer with the palm of one hand, while he held the heavy rifle in the other, like one would a pistol, and pulled the trigger. The heavy slug struck the snake, hurling it aside, while the sand thrown up from the gouge of the bullet sprayed over Uncle Pete's astonished face. The thunderous report echoed over the prairie's roll.

"Baah Jove!" he exclaimed, scrambling to his feet. "That was a close one. I never saw anything like—what did happen, anyway?"

"Shagnasty," I said, dismounting and kicking the mangled and headless snake aside, "probably saved your life. If that snake had hit you in the face . . ."

For once Pa didn't have any kidding in him for Uncle Pete.

"My God, man!" he said. "You've got to be careful, Pete. This is rattlesnake country."

"We have those back East, too," Pete said, gathering up his hat and brushing off his clothes, shaking the sand out of his beard. "I'm sure grateful, Shagnasty, that you took a good aim on that one. I wouldn't want you to have missed."

I knew then that Uncle Pete had not seen how Shagnasty had shot, one-handed, without aiming, with a weapon so heavy most men found it difficult to handle from their shoulder, shooting as he had known he had to shoot at a snake poised to strike and within striking distance. It had been, indeed, a very close thing, far closer than Uncle Pete knew.

Two hours after we left our noon stop we once again saw, far in the distance, the spot of greenery that indicated a cultivated, and probably irrigated, field of Breckenridge's Walking B Bar ranch. Pa looked at his watch.

"We're an hour ahead of where we were with the wagon," he said. "It's two o'clock now and it was three when we saw that field last fall."

"Uncle Pete," I said, pointing to the distant spot of green, "if you file on the old Box Gulch place you'll be over fifty miles from Coyote Wells but only maybe twenty miles from neighbors. That's the Walking B Bar ranch over there, lower down on the Elk from where we'll strike it."

"That's nice," Uncle Pete said with a wry grimace. "I can walk over of an evening for a game of cards."

Pa snickered.

"It's a damn cinch you won't ride no trolley car over."

Within the hour we could see, far in distance, that dark, irregular line which was the growth of box elder and cotton-wood trees which marked the contours of the flow of Elk Creek. On the rolling hills south and to our right, other distant, dark dots indicated widely scattered scrub cedar and pine. We were approaching timbered country.

When we hit our old camp ground on the Elk the sun was still two hours high above the horizon. The long, purple shadows of prairie evening had not yet begun to stretch out to the east from the low sage and to hover in the buffalo wallows which dotted the plain.

When we finally rode beneath the shade of the trees at our camp ground I felt proud of Uncle Pete. New to the saddle, he had ridden over thirty miles from the ranch. I was willing to bet that, despite the protection of his peculiarly colored chaps, the insides of his skinny legs were painfully sore and the bones of his scrawny bottom ached. And yet his only complaint was that we had purposely given him a rough-gaited horse, when actually we had given him the easiest-gaited mount on the ranch.

He sat there in his saddle with his huge hat pushed far back on his head, cocking his ear to the sound of running water, and then he rode forward to the stream, and I with him. I wouldn't have thought there could be such a change in a creek as had come to the Elk since I had last seen it. Then it had been a trickle running over the exposed bed. Now it was a lusty stream, swelled with spring's outpourings. Where before it had whispered to the shading box elders, now it fairly shouted.

"Baah Jove!" Uncle Pete exulted. "I'll bet there's fish in there. Shagnasty, where in hell did you pack my fishing tackle?"

"Fishing tackle, my eye," Pa yelled. "You better hump your back, you old coot, in making camp. These horses have got to be watered and unsaddled and unloaded and picketed, and . . ."

Pa glared around suspiciously.

"And you better watch everything you've got while we're here. There's a bunch of thievin', beady-eyed pack rats around here that will steal a person's eyeteeth. Took my pipe and tobacco and matchbox last time I was here."

Filly was tugging at her bit, wanting to go to water, so I let her, my own thirst suddenly strong in my throat. I got down and as Filly drank I lay down on my belly beside her. And then I hung there, above the water, while a cold feeling came to my spine. Before me in the clean sand were the clear prints of shod horses. I lay there, without drinking, looking at the prints as my mind sorted over the possibilities. Breckenridge riders could have ridden this way—but would they ride shod horses? Very few cowhands rode shod horses in summer on the Montana prairie. I could picture, in my mind's eye, the long, racy legs of Jed Dupre's black as it waded in to drink, sided by Steve Holden's bay. Uncle Pete was through drinking now.

"What's the matter, boy?" he asked. "Ain't you thirsty?"

"Yeah," I said, and drank, and then went to look for Shagnasty, after picketing Filly and removing her saddle. I found him starting a fire and breaking grub and tinware out of the packs that he had already removed from the pack animals.

"By Gar." He grunted. "We eat good tonight—Bullow beef."

I touched the big man's arm and as his eyes turned to

meet mine he saw what lay in them and became instantly alert.

"Down by the creek," I said. "You better read sign."

He laid down the cast-iron skillet and turned away, a huge, lumbering man who seemed to be so slow and deliberate in his movements yet could react with the speed and destructiveness of a cougar. I knew that his eyes would miss nothing along the creek and that he would read the bank like I would a printed page. I didn't want to alert Pa and Uncle Pete, perhaps falsely, so I didn't go with him, but busied myself with building the fire to a bed of coals, and helping Pa and Uncle Pete with the watering and picketing of the horses.

"Where's Shagnasty?" Pa asked. "He ain't normally one to shirk camp chores."

"Went after driftwood for the fire," I said.

He did have driftwood when he finally came back. He brought it to the fire and laid it down where I was working to lay out the canvas ground tarp and eating tinware.

"Three riders." He grunted. "One big man, two some smaller. Here three, four hours back. Toss whiskey bottle in brush. Lit out south. Two horses shod, one no iron."

I never thought for a moment to question what Shagnasty was telling me. If he said three men, instead of two men and a pack horse, that was what there had been. These men, whoever they were, were traveling light. But pack horses were not necessary here, where food bounded and ran from every covert, and the necessaries could be tied behind the saddle of each man. They could be Breckenridge's riders, but I doubted that they'd ride shod horses in summer, and, no matter what dime novels may print about it, few cowhands carried whiskey when they rode. In fact, such a practice would get a man fired on most ranches. But Jed Dupre and Steve Holden always rode shod horses—their hooves made a more elegant clatter on the streets of Coyote Wells as they rode about, showing off, attracting notice.

"They could be," I said to Shagnasty, "Jed Dupre and Steve Holden, and one of George Dupre's hands."

"Maybe." Shagnasty grunted, and his brown eyes were quiet and calm as he reached out with his huge hands to pick up a heavy stick of driftwood. Then he snapped it in two as easily as I might a match stick and smiled at me, his eyes agleam. I felt a deep surge of camaraderie for this great, shaggy, uneducated man, who had so often been with me during times of danger and never been found wanting. And there was danger now, if indeed these riders were Jed Dupre and two others, for now we were far away from Matt Fillbuster, the sheriff, and there would be no witnesses to whatever deviltry Jed might choose to cook up to harm us.

Dusk was coming down as we finished eating Bill Bullow's steak, raw fried potatoes, and Ma's home-made bread, washed down with coffee as black as tar. And with dusk came the mosquitoes. They descended on us in swarms. Shagnasty threw green wood on the fire to build a smudge as we tidied up camp and spread our bedrolls.

"Sit on the bank and fish tonight," Pa told Uncle Pete, "and you'll wind up with no blood. These skeeters will eat you up, skin and bones."

"Got 'em back East, too," Uncle Pete said, slapping one from his cheek. "They won't stop me fishin'."

They didn't. And I sat with him as he fished in the light of the lantern.

"I don't think there are any fish in this creek," I said. "It looks like there might be now, but last fall it was hardly a trickle."

"That don't cut no ice," Uncle Pete said. "When she rises in spring, fish run up her again from further down where there's more water, or maybe a bigger stream she dumps into."

"This creek," I said, "runs into the Little Missouri."

"Should be fish in her, then."

And there was. Uncle Pete managed, before the skeeters

ate him alive, to hook out two suckers and a carp, and with each fish he yelled like a Comanche Indian, and got more fun out of it than you'd think possible for a man of his age.

"What's all the racket about?" Pa yelled from his bed.

"Uncle Pete," I called back, "has caught two suckers and a carp."

"Trash fish," Pa yelled. "Ain't good for nothin'. Throw them back and come to bed. We've got a long day ahead of us tomorrow."

As I helped Uncle Pete solve the mysteries of the cowhand's bedroll tarp I thought of how this little man from back East had managed to ride a horse for thirty miles and still have enough get-up-and-go to go fishing in a cloud of mosquitoes. It appeared to me that my Uncle Pete was as tough as a pine knot.

After I got Uncle Pete snugged down in bed and had showed him how to arrange his blankets so that he could breathe without the mosquitoes biting on his long nose, I went out to visit Filly, as I had been in the habit of doing ever since she had started spending nights out with me, way back when I had been a twelve-year-old kid playing at being a cowboy. That had been seven years ago, when Filly had been a two-year-old, the most beautiful animal I had ever seen, with her strawberry-roan coat and her long, golden silver tail and mane. She heard my approach now and made that blubbering sound she always greeted me with, and I heard her picket rope slithering over the ground as she came to me. I rubbed her neck and ears and patted her sleek sides. Then I went over to where Pa had laid out his bedroll, and squatted down beside him.

"You should be in bed, son," he said.

"Wanted to talk to you a few minutes," I said.

"I see. Something on your mind?"

"Yes. There's shod horses' tracks down on the crick bank. I sent Shagnasty down to read sign and he said that there were three men, riding two shod horses and one that wasn't shod. He said one of the men was bigger than the other two and that they threw a whiskey bottle in the brush and headed on south."

"I see," Pa said. "And you think they might be some of Jed Dupre's bunch."

"They might be," I said. "They could be some of Breckenridge's riders, looking for strays. But most punchers don't ride shod horses, this time of year anyway, and knowing Breckenridge as I do, I don't picture him having riders who carry whiskey with them. He'd fire such men pronto. But one thing I am sure of, and that is that Jed Dupre and Steve Holden always ride shod horses."

"Why?" Pa asked.

"Because," I said, "the hooves of shod horses make so much more clatter when Jed and Steve cavort around the streets of Coyote Wells, showing off and trying to attract attention."

"If it is them, what are they doing here and who is the other man?"

"If," I said, "they wanted, for spite or for gain, to grab off whatever land we are after, they would bring another Dupre hand along, so that he could file on land. They'd want a man who not only could file but who would be willing to build a cabin and live on the land long enough to get a government title to it. All they'd have to do would be to dog our trail until they discovered which piece of land we were interested in and then they could mount this man on a fast horse and beat Uncle Pete to the land office."

"You could beat anything they've got on Filly," Pa said.

"Sure I could," I said bitterly, "but as you've always been fast to point out, I'm too young to file on land. And Uncle Pete couldn't make a race of it on Filly or any other horse. Besides, if Jed Dupre is running the show he'd be smart enough to see that it never came to a fair race. He'll remember that you held him up with a double-barreled shotgun and he won't be above using force. If Jed is one of those three riders, Uncle Pete has about as much chance of filing on the old Box Gulch buildings as he has of riding a bucking bronco."

"If it is Jed," Pa said, "and we are able to find out for sure that it is his bunch, maybe we could fool them. Maybe we could go on past the old Box Gulch land and on down toward the Little Cougar. In passing, Pete could get a good look at that section of land and act like he had turned it down. Then, when they got to following us down toward the Little Cougar, Pete could slip away and ride into Coyote Wells and file."

"That might work," I said dubiously.

"Well," Pa said, "there's no use staying up all night being eaten up by skeeters and chewing the fat about it. Get on to bed, son, and we'll think about it come morning."

I pulled off my pants and boots and crawled in, using my coat for a pillow and stuffing my pants in the bottom of the bedroll, where the contents of the pockets would be secure from pack rats. Pa had not seen the wild hatred flaring in Jed Dupre's eyes, as I had, when I had met him on the street in Coyote Wells. He would not be able to realize, as I did, how dangerous Dupre was, how he would do anything to avenge those six months in jail, my taking Joan away from him, the beating I had given him at the dancehall. Sleep did not come easy this night.

Even in June, at these altitudes, the nights were chilly, and the chill coming down now was sharp enough to cause the mosquitoes to go wherever they disappear to at times such as this. There was no moon in the sky, as there had been when we had camped here last. But a million stars twinkled overhead and the Milky Way arched across the world in a wide swath of awesome and mysterious beauty. The river's sullen roar seemed to be subdued now, and a coyote chorus was chanting from the ridge to the east. The last thing that I was conscious of before I dropped off to sleep was the mournful hooting of an owl, and I wondered if it could be the same owl which had greeted the night when we'd been here in October. It had been a long day.

CHAPTER SIX

When I opened my eyes in the morning there were two magpies perched on a limb, cussing me out, their white bellies and wing patches contrasting sharply with their black heads and shoulders and long, green-black tails. They were pretending to be outraged at our presence while actually keeping a sharp eye out for anything eatable that they could steal. In my kid-trapping days they had cost me many a coyote hide by disturbing my well-concealed traps, often springing them and getting caught. While Uncle Pete seemed still to be asleep, Pa was standing on his dewy tarp and hastily going through the pockets of his pants.

"Aha," he gloated, thrusting his pipe into his mouth. "I fooled 'em that time. Never got a thing off me last night."

"Maybe there's none around," I said.

"You bet your whiskers they're around. One of them galloped lickety-snort over my bed a couple times during the night. The last time I was ready for him and he didn't get away with it."

"He didn't? What did you do to him?"

"When the critter was prowling my tarp I sudden upheaved with my legs and flung the animal ten feet in the air. It made a squeaking noise and lit out like its tail was afire."

"Don't you believe that," Uncle Pete said, sitting up in his bedroll. "He wouldn't have reared up and kicked if a hippopotamus had walked over his bloody bed. He laid there, flat on his back, all night and snored. Kept me awake, he did."

Since I knew that both had slept well, because I had heard both of them snoring, I knew that they were merely back at their old game of worrying at each other, like Ma had told me they would do. A curl of smoke was coming from where Shagnasty was working with the fire and I noted that his bed was already rolled for packing. I got dressed and went to the packs for small measures of oats for each horse, rolled my bed, and then joined Pa and Uncle Pete at the fire. Shagnasty was doing his usual job of cooking and within minutes we squatted, Indian-fashion, around the ground canvas, hungrily downing stewed prunes and bacon and eggs. Shagnasty hadn't taken time to fry potatoes so we sopped up our eggs with some of Ma's bread. As we ate, a flight of ducks swooped low over the trees and then continued on north.

"Baah Jove," Uncle Pete exclaimed, "wouldn't I like a brace of those for the frying pan!"

"Couldn't hit 'em," Pa said. "Too fast for you."

"Maybe," Uncle Pete said, and a gleam of sly humor came to his expressive brown eyes. "But that Greener of mine is a powerful weapon. I recall once, when I was out with it, hunting ducks, I come upon five mallards perched on a barbed-wire fence."

Pa blew his mouthful of coffee, spraying it across the fire.

"Bobbed-wire fence!" he exploded. "No duck could sit on a wire fence. Critter's feet are flat. Wouldn't let 'em balance. They'd sort of teeter-totter and . . ."

"Bob-wire fence," Uncle Pete went on, just as though Pa wasn't there. "I sort of crouched down, so they wouldn't see me, and lined them up and let go with both barrels. Knocked off all five of them, I did. Now, the best way to cook . . ."

I looked at Shagnasty and there was absolutely no expression on his face, but deep in his eyes I could see a gleam of humor.

"Ducks," he grunted, sweeping his bread across his plate

to gather up egg yolk and then shoving the entire slice into his mouth with one deft movement, "on wire fence damned hard to hit. Good shot."

"Well, I'll be damned," Pa said in exasperation, "if you two ain't going to set there and let the old fool get away with it."

"There ain't any ducks too fast," Uncle Pete continued, "if you lead them far enough so that they run into the shot instead of having it pass behind their tails. Reminds me of the time the hurricane blew up into Massachusetts from Florida—August it was, or maybe in September. Anyway, I was out duck hunting when she hit—folks said it blew two hundred miles an hour. I was hunkered down in a hollow tree by the duck pond—you recall that pond, John, no fish in it but hell for ducks. Anyway, I was hunkered down in this hollow tree to keep from being blowed away when these ducks come streamin' through. Since the wind was blowing them at two hundred miles an hour and them flapping their wings full speed, I reckon that they was traveling all of two hundred and fifty miles per hour. . . ."

"Two hundred and fifty miles . . ." Pa echoed.

"Yeah," Uncle Pete went on. "So I just led 'em into the next county. Sam Brannigan, who lived over across the county line, maybe four, five miles, told me four of them dropped on his front porch and one went right through the living-room window."

"Broke window, eh." Shagnasty grunted.

Pa gulped the last of his coffee and got to his feet.

"Next county," he growled. "Damned if I'm going to set here wasting time, listening to any more of this."

"Now about those prunes," Uncle Pete went on, "if you could spare three or four pounds of them, and a jug, I could fix them up with a little sugar and a pinch of yeast. In a few days we'd have some powerful medicine for what ails a man. I'm a bit stiff in the joints from riding that plow horse you fellers shoved off on me."

"Why," Pa asked sarcastically, "don't you lead the damned horse into the next county, like you did them ducks."

"We'd better get rolling," I said, coming to my feet. "I figure that it is about twenty-five miles to the Box Gulch ranch buildings, maybe a bit less, and we've got the rise out of the Elk Creek drainage to climb to get over to where the land begins to slope down toward the Box Gulch Creek."

We tightened cinches and packs and led the horses to water, filled our water bags, and headed out, angling away from Elk Creek now, which we wouldn't see again until we returned. As we rode I tried to explain the lay of the country to Uncle Pete.

"When we get over the rise and to where the country begins to dip down toward the valley of the Box Gulch Creek," I explained, "you begin to notice that the sage grows higher and darker and the grass in between is heavier. Maybe they get more rain here."

Stunted pine and cedar were now scattered over the surrounding hills and choke cherry lay in low draws. On the tops of some of the jagged hills I caught glimpses of red scoria, volcanic rock, which was so common farther south near the Big Cougar River.

"That timber back along the Elk," Uncle Pete said, "was fairly respectable, but this stuff here on the hills ain't big enough hardly to fetch into the house come Christmastime."

About noon, Pa pulled Segundo back so he could talk to us.

"I'm going to stop and rest the horses while we eat a bite in a couple or three miles," he said. "Why don't you get out and shoot us some game for supper tonight."

"Fine," I said, swinging Filly to the west, where the ridge line lay about a mile distant. To the east, the top of the fold of the prairie was at least three miles away. As I approached the summit of the rise I was riding through considerable scrub cedar and pine. I dismounted just short of the top, ground hitched Filly, and walked up until I could look over the country beyond with a pair of binoculars. The glasses picked up a flash of white and when I concentrated on it the lenses brought in a small herd of antelope. They were clumped together, facing toward me as though they had been alerted. It hardly seemed to me that they had seen me, since I was concealed behind a small cedar and was barely peeking over the ridge.

I watched silently, sweeping the land with the glasses, and became more and more awed at its breadth and vast sweep, its rising and falling undulations, lonely, peaceful, and uninhabited. How fortunate I was to have been one of those who would see it thus. The timber growth was thicker here on the west slope of the rise, and after studying the lay of the land for a few minutes I got Filly and rode down the grade, studying the ground, yet alert to my surroundings. A short way down I found what I was looking for—the clear imprints of three horses, two shod, one unshod. I sat on Filly, looking down at the disturbed earth, and the vast country about me seemed no longer peaceful and uninhabited. I swept the Winchester from the saddle scabbard and levered in a cartridge, setting the hammer at half, safety cock, suddenly aware that the riders who had made these tracks might even now be sitting silently among the scrub timber, watching me, perhaps with their saddle carbines at full cock.

"No, you damned fool," I said aloud to myself, "this is the year 1915, not 1885—even Jed Dupre would not stoop to murder."

I started cautiously, following the horse sign, feeling that if these riders were slipping along, following our line of travel, but parallel to it, and just over the hill, out of our sight, they would be sure to ride up and look over from time to time to check our advance. My hunch was confirmed within a quarter mile, when the tracks turned up to the top of the rise. Here the riders had dismounted, and I could see, as Shagnasty had been able to see down on the Elk, that there were three men, and that one of them had larger feet and sank those feet deeper into the soil than his two companions.

The men evidently had squatted here and smoked cigarettes, and snuffed them out in the dirt, as all prairie-raised men do, fearing prairie fire. I carefully dug out the cigarette stubs and found that two were hand-rolled with Bull Durham tobacco and the other was a tailor-made Fatima. The quick thought came to me that Jed Dupre always smoked tailor-made cigarettes and that Steve Holden always rolled his own, probably because he couldn't afford the more expensive tailor-mades. A Dupre hired hand undoubtedly would roll his own. Not wanting to press my luck too far and risk discovery, I rode back to the trace and set Filly into the gallop to catch up with the others. Pa swiveled his horse around to meet me, holding out the little .22 rifle.

"Heck," he said, "you forgot to take this pea shooter. You can't shoot rabbits with a 30–30 saddle carbine."

"I wasn't after rabbits, Pa," I told him. "I figured that if Jed and Steve were about, they might be slipping along beside us, over that roll of hills to the west. They were, I think."

"They were," Pa echoed. "How do you know?"

"Saw their horse tracks—two shod, one unshod. They are moving parallel to our line of travel and poking their heads over now and then to check on us. One of them smokes tailor-made cigarettes and the other two roll their own."

"I see," Pa said. "So you think it is Jed?"

"I'm pretty sure."

"Well," Pa remarked, "what of it? There's no law stopping them from dogging our tracks if they take a notion, and there's nothing that we can do about it. It's a free country. I wouldn't worry about it if I were you, son."

You would, I thought, if you could have seen Jed

Dupre's eyes when he met me in town the other day.

"What do you think they are up to?" Pa asked.

"Probably, all they'll do," I said, "is follow us until they are sure what we are after, and then they'll head the man with them back to Coyote Wells on a fast horse to file on whatever land they think we want."

"And that," Pa said, "will be the old Box Gulch ranch-building section, won't it? You have your mind set on that for Uncle Pete."

"Yes."

"Maybe we can fool 'em on that. Maybe we can make believe we are simply crazy about some other section."

"We could do that," I said dubiously. "But Jed will be hard to fool. He's half crazy to get back at us, but he is also smart."

Pa glanced up at the sun.

"I'm going to pull over off the trace a way," he said, "by those trees, and we'll rest the horses a bit and eat a bite. We've got plenty of time to make the Box Gulch ranch buildings before dark, or even go on beyond them."

"All right," I said, "and while we're eating we'll tell Uncle Pete about this and discuss what we're going to do about it. In a few miles we're going to top out of this valley and get over to where the land slopes down toward the Box Gulch River, and we'd better have our plans all laid out by then, because, the way I see it, Jed and Steve are going to be close at hand."

We pulled into the scant shade of some runty cedars and loosened cinches and packs, grained the horses, built a small blaze to heat coffee, and settled back to canned beans and tomatoes, bread, and buffalo berry jam. I waited until everyone was well settled before bringing up the subject of the three mysterious horsemen.

"Uncle Pete," I said, "there's three riders following our route, just over the ridge. We spotted their tracks when we camped on the Elk and they're still with us. I think that they are Jed Dupre and his sidekick Steve Holden, and perhaps a George Dupre hired hand."

"Eh!" Uncle Pete straightened up from his slouched position. "Now what would those blighters be following us for?"

"I think," I said, "that they plan to follow us until they know what we're after down here, what land we want to file on. Then they plan to beat you to Coyote Wells and have their hired hand file on it."

"Well, I'm bedamned. Like I told you before, I ain't never set eyes on these desperadoes in my life. Why should they want to do anything to me?"

"Because," I said, "you're with us. Because you are my uncle, and any land you file on will furnish a foothold for me down here in this country. Jed Dupre would be acting merely to get revenge for my whipping him and taking his girl, and helping to send him to prison. But behind him, his father, George Dupre, probably has had his attention drawn to this fine, open range down here for the first time, and wants to grab it off, especially if while he's doing it he can get back at Pa and me for sending Jed to jail."

"I see," Uncle Pete said. "You fellers are dangerous blighters to even associate with. Man gets his ears beat down by merely having a speaking acquaintance with you. The way I see it, we might just as well turn around and go back. The minute I spot any land that looks good to me, these characters will beat me to the land office and file on it."

"You could," I said, taking a prod at Pa, "have filed on the Box Gulch section before you left Coyote Wells and had it cinched. You could have taken my word for it being what you'd like."

"You are supposed," Pa said flatly, "to have seen the land you file on. It is agen the law not to—or at least I think it is."

"I don't know about that," I said, "but we should be able

to figure some way to trick Jed—that is, if he is up to what we think he's up to."

Shagnasty had been sitting quietly, apparently not even interested in what we were talking about. But he spoke now, his voice a deep growl.

"Me stop him," he said. "Tie legs behind ears and boot in rump."

"And," Pa said, "wind up in Matt Fillbuster's jail. The best way to handle this, it seems to me, is to sort of ride across the Box Gulch section, so that Uncle Pete can get a look at it in passing, and then ride right on toward the Little Cougar River country, just like we didn't give a hoot for the Box Gulch section. Then, come dark, Pete can slip out of camp and hightail it for Coyote Wells. Time Jed and his gang knows that he is gone, he'll have a good head start."

I had a mental picture of Uncle Pete slipping out of camp and trying to beat anybody to Coyote Wells, let alone a top Dupre hand, maybe mounted on Jed's long-legged black.

"We could try that," I said, "but we'd never fool Jed by just riding by the Box Gulch buildings. That would be sure to make him suspicious that we were pulling something. He'd know that we'd be sure to stop and look over the buildings and the lay of the land, and considering that we'll get there late in the afternoon, make camp overnight. But maybe if we really take time to look the place over, maybe camp there overnight, and then pull out south in the morning, that might fool him. For all he knows, maybe we struck gold down on the Little Cougar last fall."

"I think you're right," Pa said. "If we did that, he'd be sure to follow. Then Pete could slip away at night. There isn't any moon—wasn't last night."

"That would work two ways," I said. "No moon would help Uncle Pete to get out of camp unseen, but it would also make it hard for him to find his way back to Coyote Wells. And a dark night would make it easier for Jed to get in close to our camp without being seen. If Pete is going to ride to Coyote Wells he'll have to have a long head start over Dupre's man. We'll have to really fool them."

"Right," Shagnasty said. "Like fooling Mr. Coyote. Make believe you don't see him until you get close, maybe near half a mile. Then, right in the ear."

"In the ear," Uncle Pete echoed. "At half a mile!"

"In ear best. No holes in fur that way. Get more money in St. Louis."

"What in hell are you two talking about?" Pa wanted to know. "We are supposed . . ."

"Shooting coyotes," Uncle Pete said. "I've heard the beasts yowling at night but ain't never seen one. But at half a mile—and right in the ear. Don't seem possible."

"We are supposed," Pa persisted, "to be talking about how to get the upper hand on Jed Dupre, not about shooting anybody in the ear."

"Best way," Shagnasty persisted.

"Ain't it though," Uncle Pete agreed.

"I think," I said, "we'd best get going and make the Box Gulch buildings well before dark, so we can ride around and look the section over and maybe even locate the corner markers. Then we'll make camp in the old buildings and pull out early in the morning, headed south. They are sure to follow to see what we're up to."

"But," Pa said, "we risk them shooting their man back and filing on the Box Gulch anyway."

"I'd say so," I said, "if they had more than one hired hand along. But I'm sure that neither Jed nor Steve would be willing to file on land, because that would mean they'd have to take up residence to hold it and quit hanging around Coyote Wells and George's saloon. So, they've only got one filing to make, and they won't make that until they are sure they are cutting our throats, that they are filing on something that we want. Like I said, for all they know we may have a gold mine located on the Little Cougar River."

"Sounds awfully complicated to me," Uncle Pete put in.

"Of course, I don't know the country, and Montana laws, but I've got that government rifle with me, and after riding that plow horse you set me up on way down here I ain't in no mood to have any bloody blighters prodding me around. I think that Shagnasty has the right idea—shoot in ear at half a mile."

"These men, Uncle Pete," I said, "are the kind that are apt to shoot back."

The humor left Uncle Pete's face and his eyes became serious.

"I reckon," he said. "Well, let's get on with it, shall we."

Shagnasty rose to his feet, rolled his heavy shoulders, and moved to break our noon camp. As we pulled out south our plans were made and Uncle Pete, it seemed to me, had summed it up pretty well when he said, "Let's get on with it."

Within the hour we topped the rise and started down the long slope of the prairie which was the Box Gulch Creek drainage.

CHAPTER SEVEN

Although our general line of travel was leading us down into the Box Gulch drainage it was difficult to detect that we were really going down, for the long flats of grassy sage were broken by rises, peaks, and brushy swales where rabbits ran and grouse flew. I reckoned that we had made about sixteen miles from Elk Creek when we nooned to eat and rest the horses and had made about eight miles since then. I looked at my watch; it was three o'clock. I felt a building of inner excitement because I felt that we were nearing our destination, that not too far ahead we would ride over one more of those rises and see the old buildings and the stream spread out before us. I had not been able to examine them closely the fall before because on the way down Pa wouldn't stop and on the way back we were in too big a hurry to stop. I wouldn't have been able to see them at all if it hadn't been for the runaway with Spooks and the broken reach in the wagon that we had to stop and replace.

It didn't seem to me that we would ever get there as we rode down into one draw and over the next rise. I was trying to recall just what the country had looked like before we hit the stream when I detected a quickening of Filly's pace and a forward movement of her ears.

"We're almost there," I told Uncle Pete, riding beside me. "Filly smells water."

We broke over a stiff climb and suddenly the land dropped away before us, so steeply as to be almost a cut bank. Below lay a scattering of large box elder and cottonwood trees before a long, low building, with the remains of a corral and other buildings about the yard. Beyond, the Box Gulch Creek, large enough now with spring's heavy flow to be termed a river. The stream wound through about fifty or sixty acres of lush, level meadow. From where we sat our horses I could see that the rise we were on was practically a butte, and was one of a series of buttes which stretched in an arc, so that the buildings below were protected from north winds. The old-timers had chosen this site well, for protection from the north, yet had set the buildings far enough from the buttes that they would not be drifted over from the snow that would pile up in their lee, such as we got in the lee of Pa's barn and haystack at home.

"Baah Jove," Uncle Pete's voice broke in on my thoughts. "I could irrigate that meadow down there from the brook."

"Crick," Pa said. "And you could at that. Looks better to me now than it did last fall. Let's go down and look over those buildings."

"First," I said, taking my binoculars from my saddlebag, "let's look the country over, to see if we're being watched."

"Yeah," Uncle Pete said, "if those blighters are snooping around maybe you can spot them. Maybe they're in the buildings."

"Maybe." Shagnasty grunted as he slipped his long-barreled rifle from the saddle scabbard.

"Hold it, Shagnasty," Pa snapped, his voice now holding a ring of authority. "We ain't making war on anybody. Put that rifle back where it belongs."

"What if they're down there?" Uncle Pete asked.

"What if they are," Pa said. "Maybe they'll invite us to tea. Let's get on with it."

I looked at Pa, seeing him sitting there on Segundo, broad-shouldered and solid in his saddle, his hair graying at the sides, his blue eyes now alert and sharp, speaking up, taking over command, and I felt proud to be his son. He hadn't wanted to come and had pointed out the dangers, real and imagined, but now that he was here, with Jed and his gang dogging his heels, he was once again the man I had seen walk up on a cocked Winchester in the hands of a drunken sheepherder and who had looked down the barrels of a shotgun at five armed and desperate men in a rustling camp. My pa, I thought, stands awfully tall when the cards are down.

"We'll ride down now," he said, "slow and peaceablelike. If they are there, let me handle it. If they aren't there, act like you didn't know they were about. If you see any sign, ignore it. We don't want them to know that we know they are dogging our heels."

"Your pa," Shagnasty said, as he thrust the long rifle back into the scabbard, "sly like Mr. Coyote. He fool 'em."

As we neared the buildings I could see no change in them since I had seen them last fall. The Box Gulch crew had left them in the spring of 1887, but it was known that Sandy McGovern, the ranch cook, had lived on here for several years. The buildings then had been vacant, facing the rugged Montana weather for perhaps twenty years. The house stood because it was constructed of heavy logs a foot in diameter, notched deeply at the corners. The chinking had fallen from between the logs but it was amazing how closely they had been fitted together. Red scoria rock had been laid on the low roof but was now grown up with grass and in one corner of the roof a lone cedar sapling was growing, six feet or more in height. The building seemed to be fully fifty feet long and perhaps eighteen feet in depth, with three windows with the panes of glass all broken out. Off to the side was a pole corral in bad condition and two other buildings of logs with the roofs caved in from too many winter snows.

"Big ranch, one time," Shagnasty said. "I here many times. Plenty cattle—too many cattle."

"You mean," Pa exclaimed, "that you were here in the winter of 1887!"

Shagnasty nodded and his brown eyes held a faraway look as his memories took him back to those wild, free days, when he had, perhaps, raided with or against the Sioux warriors of Two Moon. After all, he had told me that he had been a mere sprout when Sitting Bull was killed in 1881. His use of the term "sprout" didn't give much hint as to his age then, but had he been, we'll say, ten years old in 1881, he would be forty-four years old now, and sixteen when these buildings were abandoned by the Box Gulch crew. As we rode toward the buildings now Shagnasty grunted and inclined his head toward the ground and, looking down, we all saw the tracks of horses, two shod, one bare-footed.

"Ride right on," Pa said out of the corner of his mouth. "Let's see if they are home."

They weren't home. We found the heavy door unlocked and entered the building, looking it over by the light which came through the paneless windows. Except for a heavy coating of dust over everything and numerous pack-rat and mouse nests and their droppings, the place looked just as it might have looked when Sandy McGovern, the ranch cook, had left it. There was a large, combination kitchen and living room in the center and a bedroom at each end. The bedroom to the east had an old and badly rusted iron bedstead, a dresser holding a basin and pitcher, the pitcher burst open, as though it had been left with water in it and frozen. The other bedroom held a double tier of wooden bunks. The kitchen interested us the most.

The kitchen stove was on four legs with the oven door open and ashes spilling from the grate openings. On the opposite wall was a stone fireplace that looked to be in good shape yet. A chair stood by the stove with a large dishpan on it, such as one might use to raise bread for kneading. The bottom of the pan held mice droppings. A worktable was in one corner with shelves attached to the wall above. Beside the east-bedroom door stood a cabinet so tall that it almost reached to the low ceiling, the upper part two glass doors and the lower part holding drawers. A long table stood in the center of the room, hand-hewn from logs, with long benches on either side. The crew had evidently been fed here. The insides of the log walls had been hewn flat, so that had they been solidly chinked and adobe-plastered they would have been quite smooth and neat. But now one could see light between the logs where the chinking had fallen out. Our inspection was thorough but brief.

"All right," Pa said. "Let's ride out and see if we can locate the corners of this section. Try to spot piled rocks or anything which would indicate a corner marker. Shagnasty, you'd better stay and watch the pack horses. You can bring that rifle of yours in, but don't make a show of it when you do it. Pete, you'd better ride with Tom, and look the land over good—you may be owning it before long. And, boys, if you spot any men or any sign, ignore it. Just act dumb. Make believe you don't see anything."

A section of land is a mile square, with 640 acres. Locating the corners of any particular section in an area of hundred miles square is a chore for a surveyor. We didn't find any corners, but we did jump three magnificent mule deer and a bunch of antelope.

"Baah Jove," Uncle Pete breathed, "what a country. A man could shoot a winter's meat here in an hour."

We came upon a spring with many deer and antelope tracks in the mud and among them the big pad marks of a cougar, tracks I'd never forget, after our experience with one of these big cats on the trip the fall before. We came around full circle and met Pa. He hadn't found any corner markers either.

"We don't have any idea," he said, "where this section lies."

"All we have to know," I said, "is that the meadow and the stream are on the same section as the buildings. And I'm pretty sure of that."

"How come?"

"When I checked at the land office in Coyote Wells to see if the section had been surveyed and was open for filing, they had drawn these buildings in with a pen, showing their position in relation to the section lines. It appeared to me that the north line laid just to the north of that rise we came over when we saw the buildings, and that the buildings laid at about the center of the north line. This would put about three quarters of a mile of ground to the south of the buildings and this would take in the meadow for sure. The stream runs through the full width of the land, west to east."

"In that case," Pa said, "we'll just take a chance that whoever drew that tracing on the township map knew what he was doing. Pete, do you reckon you want this land badly enough to live fifty miles from town?"

"You bet," Uncle Pete said enthusiastically. "It would be a big job, but give me some teams and machinery and maybe a hired hand or two and it would work out. I'd dig a ditch to that meadow and put in alfalfa."

"And," Pa said, "milk cows and haul milk and cream fifty miles to Coyote Wells."

"Beef stuff will eat alfalfa," I reminded Pa. "Bill Bullow grows it."

"Yeah. Well, let's head for the buildings and see if we can shake together some groceries. How the hell are we going to sleep in that place with all those mice and pack rats?"

"I'm not," I said. "I'm going to unroll my bed beside that creek, where I can hear the water sing all night. That's the most wonderful sound in the world."

When we returned to the camp we found that Shagnasty had unsaddled Big Red and the pack horses and picketed them in the lush graze of the meadow, and lugged packs and saddles inside. The big man was up on the low roof with a long pole, shoving it down the stove's chimney.

"Pack-rat nests," he said. "Big smoke inside unless I poke out."

He came down, started a fire in the kitchen stove, and broke out grub and dishes from the packs.

"Sprout," he complained, "didn't shoot rabbits. So we eat bacon and spuds."

The stove drew well and the fire crackled. I looked longingly at the fireplace, which seemed to be in pretty good shape, wishing for a fire there. Pa called a conference as we ate.

"Now," he said, "we've looked over the land and Pete wants to file on it. In the morning we'll saddle up and head south toward the Little Cougar River country, just like we didn't care for this place. Then, tomorrow night we'll make camp and Pete will sneak off to Coyote Wells to file."

"Maybe," I said, "either me or Shagnasty should go with him."

"Perhaps," Pa said, "but it would make it harder to fool them. Pete has to have a long head start. Now I've got it figured out that we can arrange our big tarp over a tree limb so it will be like a tent. Then the three of us can move in and out, maybe changing clothes, such as one of us putting on this big hat of Pete's, and make them think that there are still four of us in camp. That way they may not get wise that Pete is gone for a long time."

"Bosh!" Uncle Pete exclaimed. "I can't see any reason for all this fooling around. Looks like foolishment to me. It seems to me that all we have to do is to saddle up and ride back to Coyote Wells. Sure, we've seen some horse tracks, but we don't know who made them, and nobody has bothered us in any way. These riders could be just some sneak thieves, hanging around in hopes of stealing some of our gear. I think that you blighters have got yourselves all wound up in imagining things."

"Maybe," I said. "But if we start riding toward Coyote Wells and that is Jed Dupre's outfit out there, we will have announced to them that this is the land we came to see and this is the land we are going to file on. They'll head for town and file on it before we can get there."

"If that is so," Uncle Pete argued, "you tell me that this Filly horse of yours is the fastest in the country. All you have to do is ride on ahead and beat them to it."

"Tom," Pa reminded him, "is too young to file, and he can't file for you."

"Well then," Uncle Pete said, "I'll ride the critter myself."

"You," Pa countered, "couldn't beat the slowest horse in the Dupre remuda, if it was ridden by a Dupre top hand."

"Well now, I don't know about that, John."

"I do," I said flatly. "And if I know Jed Dupre's style and the way he thinks and the ruthless way he acts, he wouldn't let you get started if you tried to move out north in the morning. And if you tried to move out now he'd be watching and stop you. But if we go south in the morning he won't be looking for you to double back. Now, if we're going to bed down in here we'd better take the horses off the picket lines and tie them in close to the house."

Right," Pa said. "We don't want to wake up come morning and find ourselves afoot. And we'd better set a guard during the night."

"Foolishment," Uncle Pete scoffed.

"Little friend damned fool," Shagnasty rumbled. "Me stand guard."

Uncle Pete turned to study Shagnasty's face and his eyes became doubtful. Pete thought a lot of Shagnasty's opinions.

We wanted to leave the horses on the lush grass as long as possible, being shy on grain, so we didn't move to take them in until darkness was coming down. There were two bracketed lamps attached to the cabin walls and we had kerosene for our lantern, so we were able to get the lamps functioning. The old room took on a homey glow in their light. I was just starting to rise from one of the benches at the table where we were sitting when Jed Dupre stepped through the door, closely followed by Steve Holden and another man. Jed held a Winchester carbine in his hands and the room was so quiet that I distinctly heard the click as he cocked back the hammer. The lethal muzzle moved back and forth over us.

"Now, you bastards," he gritted out, "the shoe is on the other foot. Make a move, damn you, and I'll blow your heads off."

I slowly sat down again, with my hands flat on the table, hoping that no one would make a false move. This big, heavy-shouldered, black-eyed man would shoot—I could see it in his eyes.

"You're crazy, Jed," I said.

An expression of disgust lay across Pa's face and, as usual, Shagnasty's features held no hint of what he was thinking. Only Uncle Pete reacted.

"So," he said, "these are the bloody snakes in the grass you blighters have been talking about."

"Shut up," Jed said, swiveling the rifle to cover Uncle Pete, while Steve and the other man sidestepped with leveled handguns.

"You only got six months, Jed," Pa remarked, "the last time. So far you've earned about two years. Yank that trigger and you hang. Now you better back off and tell us what you have on your mind. Put those guns down. None of us are armed."

And we weren't armed. Shagnasty's rifle leaned in a far corner. My rifle and Pete's were in the scabbards on our saddles, also piled in the corner. And Pa's shotgun was there on one of the packs, as was the little .22 rifle.

"Lucky you're not armed," Steve Holden boasted. "We'd just love to shoot it out with you."

"You," I told him, "have got a yellow stripe up your back, Steve, as wide as my two hands."

I looked at the other man now, trying to place him, to

judge him, so that I might know what to expect of him. He was about my size, though somewhat heavier through the chest and some older, a solid, brute-jawed individual with pale, almost yellow eyes, and a week's growth of whiskers, his lower lip pooched out with snoose, which showed brown on his lips. He looked back at me with a sort of devil-may-care expression, and I knew then that he would be a far more dangerous adversary than Steve Holden.

"Jack Stockman," he said, "and I ain't pleased to meet you."

"All right," Pa said flatly, "you've got us cold, Dupre. Now what's your game?"

"You want this section of land," Dupre said, "and so does my father. So, we hold you here tonight while Jack rides to Coyote Wells and files on it. He should make it by morning if he starts now."

"And then," Steve said, tossing his yellow forelock out of his eyes, "we beat the living daylights out of you for sending us to jail and then let you walk back to town."

"Walk?" Uncle Pete echoed.

"Yes," Jed snapped. "Jack, go out there and cut those picket ropes and chouse those animals off to the north. They'll drift back to their home range and these jokers can walk it. After you do that, head out for Coyote Wells and file. There won't be anybody following you."

We sat there, helpless under their guns, listening to their man yelling as he turned the horses loose and headed them out north. Then he appeared in the still-open door and raised a hand to Jed in farewell.

"I'm off," he said. "See you in Coyote Wells."

"You won't dare go to Coyote Wells, Jed," Pa said. "Matt Fillbuster will toss you in jail and throw away the key."

"Why?" Jed's coal-black eyes held a sly look of triumph. "We haven't done anything but ride down here to find some land for one of my cousins to file on. It isn't our fault if you got careless and let your horses stray, or maybe they got spooked off by a cougar."

"Fillbuster won't buy that," Pa said, "especially not from a jailbird."

"Jailbird," Jed hissed, and he came across the room like a panther, with the rifle barrel poised to strike Pa. But Shagnasty started to rise from the bench and Jed saw his danger and drew back, no doubt recalling the speed and deadliness of Shagnasty's attack in the rustling camp.

"Tie them up, Steve," Jed ordered. "Get rope from their saddles there."

He swung the muzzle of the rifle back and forth.

"Move to the far wall. Face it with your hands over your heads and flat against the wall. If you try any funny business I'll shoot and claim self-defense."

"Self-defense," Pa hooted as we moved to face the wall, "with an unarmed man shot in the back. You'd hang, Jed."

The quick thought came to me that this remark of Pa's was bound to have an effect on Jed. Even gripped by the wild, insane rage, as he was, he would not dare shoot a man in the back. He'd hesitate with Pa's remark fresh in his mind. This might stay his trigger finger long enough . . . long enough for what? I could picture Jack Stockman riding for Coyote Wells and I could also picture that beautiful stream out there, with the lush meadow, and Joan and I owning it, or at least living here with Uncle Pete. Steve Holden was moving, with pieces of rope in his hands, stepping up to Pa beside me. I knew that once we were tied that was an end to it and the thought drove me berserk. I whirled, staggering Steve aside with my shoulder as I dove long and low for Jed's legs. I saw the rifle barrel coming down, heard the thunderous report in the room, felt the burning of the bullet along my back. And then I had my arms around Jed's legs. I heard Steve's loud yell, "Back there or I'll shoot," and then Jed went sprawling aside and his legs were free of my arms. I saw him twisting like a cat, swinging the rifle around, levering in a cartridge as he did so. I saw the empty brass flung across the room by the rifle's action, even as I dove through the open door into the darkness beyond, running full-tilt away.

"Let him go, Jed," I heard Pa yell. "The kid's too young to file on land."

The rifle crashed behind me and I saw the flame lancing from the muzzle, reaching for me, and I heard the slug strike the ground beside me and then go buzzing away into the night. I dove to the ground, rolled aside, and then was up and running again.

"Watch it, Jed," I heard Steve scream, and I was too far into the darkness to be shot at anymore.

I made a wide turn around the light of the buildings to come to the steep rise behind them, knowing that they could not take up any chase after me because they would have to keep Pa and Shagnasty covered and tie them up—a dangerous job with Shagnasty. And there was something else that I knew, something that Jed Dupre wouldn't know because he was not the type of man to have anything like this in his mangy life—the deep affection of his horse. I knew that Big Red, even Segundo, and the pack horses, would head out north, toward the home range, perhaps feeding as they went, taking days to do it, but surely going. Segundo might stay if he thought he was expected to, but after being cut loose from his picket rope and choused north by Stockman, Segundo would go. But Filly would not. She would not leave me. I was as sure of this as I was certain that between us, man and horse, lay a bond that would be completely beyond Jed Dupre's understanding.

I thought about what might be happening at the cabin and considered going back and snooping around. But there had been only two shots fired, and both fired at me. So Pa and Uncle Pete had not been shot, and neither had Shagnasty been able to gain the upper hand during the confusion caused by my escape, for if he had they would now be calling out to me. Therefore, I reasoned, they were still held under Jed's guns.

I began walking up the steep butte behind the buildings. It was pitch dark and I found myself stumbling over scrub sage and into brush. At the top I stopped and listened for long moments and then I heard movements off to my left and called out softly, "Filly." The soft, blubbering sound that Filly always made in greeting came back to me from the darkness. I couldn't see her, but held out my hand and crooned to her and she came and laid her nose in my palm, and I put my arms around her neck and tears rolled down my cheeks, and I was not ashamed, for they were tears of relief, and of affection for this golden mare that had shared my life these many years and was forever faithful.

CHAPTER EIGHT

Jack Stockman had known what he was doing when he had cut Filly's picket rope. He'd cut it just long enough so that she wouldn't step on it and still long enough that it would hit the ground as she walked, and so fray out the end to conceal the fact that it had been cut with a sharp knife. I stood now, crooning to my golden, strawberry-roan mare, stroking her neck beneath the long mane, wondering just what I should do now.

The best thing to do, it seemed to me, was head for Coyote Wells and get Matt Fillbuster, the county sheriff, in on this deal. Jack Stockman couldn't be more than a half hour ahead of me, and Jed had assured him that there wouldn't be anybody following him. Therefore, he wouldn't be driving his mount hard, and I was pretty sure that, riding Filly bareback, I could beat him into town. But if I did this, could I stop Stockman from filing? After all, it was Jed and Steve Holden who were holding Pa and Shagnasty and Uncle Pete at gunpoint, not Stockman. Fillbuster was an honest lawman, but he did obey the law, and if he stopped Stockman from filing, and Uncle Pete later got the land, Stockman would be, possibly, in a position to sue Fillbuster.

Then again, the land, though very important in this, was not as important as getting the others out from under Jed's guns. The sharp pain in my back, behind the left shoulder, the feeling that my shirt was stuck to my back with drying blood, made me realize that Jed actually would shoot, and to kill. I grabbed the cut picket rope, my decision made, mounted Filly, and headed out for Coyote Wells. I let her walk easy until we were beyond hearing and then struck out at the lope. I felt no uneasiness about being chased because I knew that Jed and Steve dare not leave to take after me, and I did not want them to know that one horse had not strayed and that I was mounted and therefore a danger to them—how I could be a danger I had not yet figured out.

Filly had gone twenty-five miles this day, but she had been picketed on lush grass for four hours, and had been fed oats. Running her flat out the fifty miles to Coyote Wells would bring me a dead or at least wind-broken horse. But by alternately walking, trotting, and loping I felt that I could make it without doing her any permanent harm. It was very dark, but I could see fairly well in the starshine, and Filly could see much better, as she proved as she threaded her way down the trace, through scrub timber, sage, draw, and gulley. I rode with my mind chewing on a problem which would not be solved merely by beating Jack Stockman to Coyote Wells.

As I progressed a plan began to form in my mind which was so audacious that it brought shivers up my wounded back. Could I pull this off? I asked myself. Just how much did Joan Bauer actually care for me? Would she hesitate, stall for time, be bewildered by it all, lose the precious seconds, or would she, as she had done that day in the Prestons' kitchen, cock her head on one side, tinkle with laughter, and say, "Tom, anytime you say." The thought had hit me fully now, as a reality, not something to just dream about and wish for, that if I could marry Joan before Jack Stockman could arrive in Coyote Wells, I could file on the land, regardless of my age, as the head of a family. As Filly loped along I kept turning this over in my mind, realizing that everything would depend on two factors, these being my arrival in Coyote Wells at least a half hour ahead of Stockman, and Joan being willing to instantly cooperate with me.

A wedding, I knew, meant many things to a woman, long

preparation, new dresses, invitations to friends, showers, and what have you. Could I then rush up to the Preston residence on a lathered horse, charge into the Preston kitchen, grab Joan by the hand, and tell her that she had to rush to the courthouse with me and marry me so that I could beat a character whom she had never heard of to some land that she had never seen and probably never wanted to see? After all, she had not seen the Box Gulch River threading its way through that lush meadow. It seemed to me that Joan might back off and say, "Tom Conway, you're out of your mind."

Riding bareback was, for me, as easy as riding a saddle. I rode Filly a good share of the time bareback. I was so expert at it that I could, and had, when wanting to show off a bit, picked up a handkerchief from the ground at the gallop. It was an easy trick once you knew how to do it, using your downward momentum to help your upward return; like the bouncing of a ball, you bounced your body. And Filly, without the added weight of a saddle, could, I knew, run anything Stockman happened to be riding right into the ground. Although my mission, as I saw it, was to reach Matt Fillbuster, I might be able to scoop up the land while I was about it without losing any time and without further endangering Pa and Uncle Pete and Shagnasty. Filly began trying to swerve off to the right so I pulled her up and sat there, listening, and I heard the musical whisperings of the Elk—we had come this far, twenty-five miles.

I lit a match and looked at my watch. It was one o'clock. Since I had little idea of when we had started out, I had no way of knowing how many miles we had averaged per hour. I rode Filly to the Elk and let her drink, pulling her away before she'd had her fill, thinking of the time and when we could arrive in Coyote Wells. Then a new thought struck me. If I rode on I could possibly arrive in five more hours— six o'clock. And the courthouse and the land office would not open until nine o'clock. I sat down, lay back, and looked at the stars. Good Lord, I had time to waste. And so had Jack Stockman. And then I knew this wasn't so. For me the courthouse would open at nine o'clock; but for Stockman, anytime George Dupre told it to open, for George had put most of the men working there into office. Joan had warned me of this, of George Dupre's influence in Coyote Wells. The answer to this one, it seemed to me, was that I would have to be in Coyote Wells when the courthouse opened but Jack Stockman would have to be someplace else. This was an unpleasant thought and one that gave me a hollow feeling in my belly, since Stockman was armed and I was not. I wondered what Pa would do in a situation like this. Charging forward with one's Callahan blood aroused, in this instance, might only result in a bullet in the chest.

My best chance, it seemed to me, was to in some way get ahead of Stockman, and lie in wait for him along the trace, which he'd surely be following. I might beat him into town but not by enough time—I had to delay him further. I rode Filly back to the trace, knowing when she hit it by the way she struck out at a fast canter, sure of her footing. Daylight comes early in Montana in June, and I knew that it would be getting light around four. I felt that I was close behind Stockman by now and didn't want to ride up on him unknowingly in the dark. I wanted to see him first, to swing wide around him.

The whole idea seemed an impossible task and I felt apprehension rising within me, and cold, clammy fear, and my back was beginning to hurt like hell. I hadn't taken time to try to find out just how much damage Jed's bullet had done —a man can't very well look over his shoulder in the dark. But the wound was no longer bleeding and this gave me some comfort.

Dawn began to bring light to the east, beginning with that faint, ever-growing glow, and the tiny birds in the sage began to chirp. I mounted a rise where I could see the trace far ahead, and there was no rider on it and I felt sure that in some way I had passed Stockman. I pulled up, sat there, my pants clinging to my legs with Filly's sweat, and got the break I needed. Ahead, off to the right, a thin spiral of smoke rose from a heavy clump of sage.

We were not over five miles out of Coyote Wells now, and there was no timber about here to hide a man and horse. I could picture Stockman, sure of himself, thirsting for coffee after the all-night ride, pulling off into heavy sage where he could find fuel for a fire, and breaking out his canteen of water and his pot and brewing something that no rider denies himself if it is available. I rode Filly down into a gully, ground hitched her, and started sneaking up on the thread of smoke.

Many years when the only firearm I had owned was the little, single-shot .22 rifle had taught me the fine art of slipping up on game. Many a coyote, the wariest animal of the plains, had been surprised to find me in close range after crawling over almost open terrain. But now I not only had to fool Stockman, I also had to fool his horse. Let his mount have its attention drawn by a suspicious movement in the sage, so that it looked my way intently, ears cocked forward, and a man such as I took Stockman to be would be on to me in a flash.

Such an approach cannot be hurried. It requires the most infinite care and patience, selecting the route ahead, slithering from one sage clump to the next. One must not snap a twig, or cause a sage to rustle in a way that it would not rustle with the wind. I had to go slowly, and yet I feared that at any moment Stockman might finish his coffee, stamp out his fire, mount his horse, and see me lying there, flat on my face. It seemed to me to be an hour before I was close enough, and in proper position to see the man. He was sitting with his back toward me, but just enough on a bias that I could see the coffee cup in his hand. His horse was tied beyond to a clump of sage, a rangy bay, gathering what browse it could. The animal would lower its head to get a mouthful of grass and then lift it as it contentedly chewed. I began to time my movements to the time when the horse had its head down, its vision blocked by sage.

I was within twenty feet of Stockman when he suddenly sensed my presence and turned his head to see me. When I saw recognition come to his yellow eyes I leaped up and charged toward him. He had his Colt halfway out of the holster when I gripped his wrist and drove my knee upward into his crotch with all my force. He howled in agony and tried to pull away from me. This gave me a shot at his chin with my fist. I'd never fought a man but twice in my life—when I fought Jed at the dancehall the first time I'd taken Joan out, and when I fought again in the rustler's cabin last fall. I may not know how to properly hit a man or be expert at it, but when my fist connected with Stockman's jaw I could feel the jolt of it clear to my shoulder and the force of it tore my shirt loose from my wound and I could feel warm blood coursing down my back again as I lowered Stockman to the ground, out like a snuffed candle.

I laid the man down, dragged him back against a sage clump, unbuckled his gunbelt, and strapped it around my middle, feeling a bit foolish about this, for Pa had always been dead set against me wearing a sidearm, and I knew that I was no great shakes at using one. I went to Stockman's horse and got his Winchester and cradled it in my arm, and put two fingers in my mouth and blew a signal to Filly. Then I sat down and drank some of Stockman's coffee while I watched full consciousness come to him. He leaned there, half sitting, against the sage clump, his yellow eyes staring at me, cold as ice.

"You hit hard, kid," he said.

"You'd have shot me," I said, "if you could."

"I would," he said, "and I will, the next time I see you. And you'd better be armed when we meet."

"Come off it, Stockman," I said. "This is 1915, not 1857. You're too young a man to be trying to live in the past that ain't here anymore. When you meet me again I won't be swaggering around wearing a gun like a Sears and Roebuck cowboy or an imitation Billy the Kid. I'll be un-armed, and if you shoot me you'll hang, and if you tackle me without shooting me I'll beat your damned head off. Now where do we go from here?"

I suddenly realized that I was talking as Pa might talk if he were in my shoes, and felt some pride in it.

"You tell me," he said sullenly. "I'm just a hired hand for George Dupre."

"But riding with his son. Well, you were headed for Coyote Wells to file on some land for George Dupre, but in your name, that my uncle planned on filing on, but because George Dupre was paying you to do it you were in the wrong and I was in the right."

"What good did it do for you to tackle me? You're too young, they tell me, to file on land yourself. You haven't gained anything by slowing me up."

"I know," I said, not wanting him to know what I planned to do.

"Well then," he went on, "it seems to me that you're in a bad fix, kid. You sneak up on my camp and knock me cold. I can have you arrested for battery and assault, and don't think that George Dupre can't make it stick. I can have you sent to prison for five years. The best thing for you to do is beat it, kid."

I turned my head to see Filly approaching, holding her head way off to one side so that she wouldn't step on the grounded reins and hurt her mouth. Stockman saw her.

"So," he said gustily, "your horse didn't drift north—you've got a trained animal there."

"I've got an animal," I said sarcastically, "that loves me. Did anything, human or animal, ever love you, Stockman?"

Now that I had Stockman I didn't know what to do with him. I could sit here looking at him until it was nearly time for the courthouse to open and then tie him up and leave him. I began to mentally cuss myself for not tying him when

he was unconscious. I could tie him up and leave for
Coyote Wells now, and have time to talk to Joan, to make
her see things as I saw them. Stockman wasn't doing any
swearing or raving or making any wild threats, and this, to
me, made him a more dangerous man, one who might try to
lull me into a feeling of security by his very calmness. I
knew that it would be very dangerous to try to tie him up
alone. In the twinkling of an eye he could turn the tables on
me. I didn't want to do him any more damage than I had already done, for I was really worried about his threat to have
me arrested and thrown in jail. His charges, after holding us
up at the Box Gulch camp with Jed, would seem to be utterly ridiculous, but with George Dupre backing him they
might stick. I had been able to talk like Pa, but could I act
like he would now—wisely? I looked at my watch. It was
seven o'clock.

"What are we going to do," Stockman asked, "just set
here? The longer you hold me here the worse it is going to
be for you when I have you arrested."

"Relax," I said. "Just relax."

We sat there, facing each other across the dead fire's
ashes as the sun rose higher and higher and the
meadowlarks sang from the sage clumps, and winged aloft
and sang there, and hawks soared on still wings against the
blue of the sky, and a bunch of antelope came close and got
our scent and stampeded away, only to turn and look back,
their white rump hairs flashing the danger signal. It was
restful, after riding all night, and my eyes were weary.

"The trouble with greenhorns like you," Stockman said,
"not yet dry behind the ears, is that you ain't got the guts to
shoot a man. Sure, you don't go around armed, because you
might have to use a gun if you wore one. You've got two
guns now, and you wouldn't use them even if I jumped
you."

This snapped me wide awake.

"You think not. Try it, Stockman."

I looked at my watch again and it was eight-thirty. Good Lord, had I dozed off and didn't know it? I got to my feet and backed away from Stockman, the rifle ready, and got hold of the reins of his horse and then led her to Filly. I stuck Stockman's rifle in his saddle boot and swung up on Filly. Filly turned in to me, as she always does, and when I straightened up Stockman was gone. He had rabbited off into the sage. I galloped forward and saw him running down into the draw, and started to go after him. Then I pulled up. Maybe this was the best solution. I could reach Coyote Wells in half an hour and he couldn't possibly get there for an hour afoot. This would give me the edge I needed, a precious half hour. I jerked Stockman's horse into a gallop beside me and headed across country for Coyote Wells by the shortest route I knew. I had my half hour. But would it be enough?

CHAPTER NINE

I took Stockman's gunbelt off and stuffed it in his saddlebag and turned his horse loose, just out of town. I didn't want anything of his on me, so that he could claim that I had robbed him. Then I rode in, avoiding downtown, hitting the street where the Prestons lived and tying Filly in the alley. When I dismounted my knees were trembling with the tension that was now a part of me. Tackling Stockman with a mad bull-like rush wasn't going to hold a candle to tackling Joan in the Prestons' kitchen, with the tale I had to tell. I guess a man wonders, even after he's been married to a woman for years, just how much she really cares for him, just how far she would really go for him. I knew that what I was about to do was going to make Joan look ridiculous, any way you looked at it, and this was something I didn't want to do, dreaded doing. But I finally got up nerve enough to walk across the yard and knock on the door, not realizing how I must look, with three days' growth of beard, my face dirty from crawling through the sage, my clothing full of sand and cockle burrs. But this didn't seem to make any difference to Joan.

"Tom," she trilled as she opened the door, and flung herself into my arms. "When did you get back?"

I was kissing her when I felt her stiffen and draw away, and then she stepped back, looking at her bare arms, which were stained with dark, dried blood.

"Tom!" she cried out. "You've been hurt."

She spun me around and I guess the bullet must have

made an awful-looking mess of my back, because I heard her gasp.

"Get that shirt off," she said, turning swiftly to get a clean cloth from a drawer and to pour hot water from the stove into a wash basin.

"Joan," I said, "there's no time for that! There's no time."

"No time," she cried, her eyes fearful. "My God, Tom, you've been shot!"

"Just a scratch," I told her, reaching out to take her by the shoulders.

"Listen, Joan. There's no time. We've got to get to the courthouse. We've got to get married—fast."

"What? Why?"

"So I can be the head of a family and able to file on land. Jack Stockman, a Dupre hand, will be here in just a few minutes to file on the Box Gulch land. I'm not twenty-one. I can't file unless you marry me."

"I see," she said, and her dark eyes became angry. "So I'm to marry you so that you can get land. Is that it, Tom? Well, I won't do it."

"No, Joan!" I cried out. "You'll be marrying me to get our land, our home. You'll be marrying me because I love you, because we love each other."

"Love," she said, and the anger went from her eyes and they became soft and shining and beautiful. "Love, Tom. Of course. Let me get my hat and change my—"

"There's no time for a hat," I cried, and then I had her by the hand and was taking her out the door and hoisting her on Filly, so fast that I doubt if she realized that there was no saddle. Straddling a horse bareback, without a riding skirt, exposes a girl's legs more than folks generally think they should be exposed, so that those we passed got an eyeful of a pair of very beautiful legs. Joan was protesting and trying to pull her dress down but it didn't do her much good because we were at the courthouse and I had her off of Filly and was hustling her up the steps, talking as fast as I could, trying to explain to her about Stockman and Pa and Uncle Pete and Shagnasty and Jed Dupre, and my need for speed and Matt Fillbuster, and how I hoped that George Dupre wouldn't be awake yet and try to interfere. I didn't think that she was getting a word of it, but she was all right.

"Tom, Tom," she said as we went up the courthouse steps, "stop it. You don't need to explain to me. I'm with you and I'll always be with you. Now where the hell do we get that marriage license?"

Hearing Joan say "hell" knocked all the hysterics out of me and I steered her right up to the long counter before the county clerk and recorder's desk. I knew the man, Bert Jonas, and he knew me, and I knew that he had once kept books for George Dupre. He was a small man, about thirty-five, with the kind of face that seems to be telling you that he feels that he is a little bit above you, that you are a little bit below his level.

"What can I do for you, Tom?" he asked.

"We want a marriage license."

He looked at Joan.

"Yes," she said, blushing.

"I see," he said hesitantly. "But, Tom, you are not of age. You will require parental consent. That means that you will have to have one of your parents sign for you."

"I know what the word means," I snapped, standing there with my world collapsing around my ears.

And then a huge hand gripped my shoulder.

"Hell, if it ain't Tom Conway. Didn't know you was back yet until me and Dennis saw you unload in front—where the hell's your saddle? I been takin' care of your Ma's needs while you been gone. She and Rose Shagnasty are in town with us right now."

I turned to look into the smiling face of Mike Flaherty, and beside him stood his brother, Dennis.

"Capital!" Dennis exclaimed.

"Dennis," I said, "get out of here and bring Matt Fillbuster just as fast as you can."

"Capital," Dennis said as he turned away. "I'll get him, Tom."

Mike trotted to the door and stuck his head out and yelled loud enough to be heard clean across town.

"Hey, Ma—Mrs. Shagnasty—Tom's back."

The last thing I wanted everybody to know was that I was back. George Dupre worked nights and slept days, but Mike's bellow could even raise the dead. Hardly before I knew what was happening, Ma was there and Rose Shagnasty was there and I was engulfed in both their arms.

"What on earth happened to you, boy?" Rose wanted to know. "You look like you been dragged backward through a cactus patch."

She spun me around.

"Lord love us, Ma, the boy's been shot, or something. Look at his back. Shirt's tore open and blood all over."

I fought her off and I fought Ma off, them wailing about the back needing care and where was Pa and Uncle Pete and Shagnasty.

"Ma," I yelled, "for God's sake, listen to me and stop asking questions. Joan and I have got to get a marriage license and get married fast. And this damned clerk won't give it to us unless you sign for it."

"Good gracious," Rose said, reaching out now to engulf Joan in her ample arms and patting her soothingly on the back. "Now don't you fret about it, honey—it happens in the best of families sometimes, although I wouldn't have expected it of Tom—he's so shy."

"What," Joan cried out, jerking free of her, "are you talking about? If you think I'm pregnant . . ."

"Pregnant," Ma cut in, her hand flying up across her mouth. "Oh, dear me . . ."

"Ma," I yelled, grabbing her with one hand and reaching

across the counter to grab the clerk with the other hand and practically ramming them together, "we need that marriage license. We need it fast. And you sign for it fast."

Ma turned and looked at me, her eyes probing mine deep and searchingly, and then she smiled.

"Yes, Tom," she said. "Of course. Mr. Jonas, if you'll be so kind as to make out the necessary papers I'll sign them."

The clerk hesitated, no doubt thinking about what Jed Dupre might do to him for making out a marriage license for me to marry Joan Bauer. And while he hesitated a brawny hand shot across my shoulder and grasped him by the shirt front and lifted him clear off the floor, and I was pushed aside and Mike Flaherty stood there with a fist the size of a picnic ham poised under Jonas's nose.

"Hell," Mike roared. "Didn't you hear the man? Are you going to stand there flat-footed or are you going to make out that license, or am I going to flatten your silly nose all over your silly face. Mother of God . . ."

Jonas's face was blue and his heels were in the air and he was squirming and he was scared.

"Let him down, Mike," I said.

"All right," Mike said, lowering the man and releasing his shirt. "But by the Holy Mother, if that piece of paper ain't slid across that counter in thirty seconds I'll . . . why, damn it, man, this lady has to get married. . . ."

Joan stamped her foot in anger.

"I don't have to get married," she wailed. "I just want to so Tom can . . . oh, Tom, they don't seem to understand."

"I don't give a hoot whether they understand or not," I said as the clerk handed me the license and I handed him the two dollars. "Now where is somebody who can marry us?"

"Hell, there ain't that much of a rush, is there, Tom?" Mike asked, looking Joan's slim figure up and down. "A person wouldn't think it from looking at—"

"Mike," I cried out, "for God's sake, a minister, a justice of the peace, a judge, anybody."

"Them," Mike declared, "is the only ones you can use, except of course if you was at sea."

"He's at sea all right," Rose Shagnasty said, grasping me by the arm. "Come along, Joan, I'll steer you to the right place. I been there myself, when I hitched up with Shagnasty, so I know right where it is."

She opened a door and we all surged in like stampeding cattle in a branding chute. It was the same room where I had appeared as a witness against Jed and Steve when they had their trial for stealing our cattle. As we entered, as I found out later, Judge Harvey Stark was trying to settle an affair of fisticuffs between the town drunk, Peter O'Brian, and Ross Shultz, a farmer who liked his beer a bit too well, without having to throw either one of them in jail. Shultz, it seemed, was being a bit difficult. He stood before the judge's desk, teetering on his heels and glaring around like a half-stupefied and very indignant owl. O'Brian was apparently out on his feet.

"This shmaltz," he declared, "this verdamned stuffed sausage, vollop me on mine nose—der snoot. I vollop him in der brisket und—Himmel—in my face he spitten."

"I know, I know," the judge said, "in der face spitten—I mean—well, he told me that you spit in his beer."

"In der beer, nein. I miss. Den in der snoot he bash und . . ."

"To hell with you damned snoot," Mike cut in. "Judge, Tom here and this lady—Joan Bauer—are in a rush to get married. It seems that . . . hell, anyway . . ."

"What in time's going on here anyway?" the judge thundered, his silver-white mustache fairly bristling with indignation. "Isn't it enough that I have to endure these two drunks without a damned Irisher barging in—oh, Mrs. Conway, Mrs. Shagnasty, Miss Bauer. I beg your pardon, but what is going on here?"

Ma came forward there, in her gentle way, good breeding in her every word and gesture.

"Please," she said quietly, "will you marry my son, Tom, to Miss Bauer? They have the license. There has been some trouble—it is necessary and very urgent. I don't know, but—please."

The judge's piercing gray eyes studied Ma's face for a moment and then he turned to the two drunks.

"Out," he said, "and if you come before me again I'll have you locked up and throw away the key. Mr. Conway, Miss Bauer, will you please step this way and join hands. . . ."

Such a wonderful and awesome thing to take place in such a few minutes, a man and a woman bound together as man and wife with a few simple words and a sheet of paper. I don't remember the first part of it because I was practically unconscious, but I'll always remember the last, loud and clear, when Judge Stark's voice rolled sonorously over the room and he intoned, "By the power vested in me I now pronounce you man and wife."

And then, once again, we were engulfed with well-wishers, with questions from those who did not understand the urgency, the judge, and even the two drunks, who had hung around to see the ceremony. I kissed Joan and she clung to me, even as I was urging her out of the room.

"The land office," I hissed. "Across the hall—quickly!"

"Yes, yes, Tom," Joan gasped.

What a hell of a way to get married, I thought.

"Hell," Mike was at my elbow again, "what's the hurry now? Everything's tied up nice and legal."

"Mike," I said, "stay with me. Clear the way to the land office. I've got to file on section six, township—do you see Dennis and Fillbuster around?—I need him—yes, Ma, Pa's all right I guess. Don't ask me questions now, I've got to file on . . ."

We were in the land office now and I was facing

paunchy, bald-headed Henry Engle across his desk. I managed to get it out now, section, township, and range, and it was right and he knew it was right, and he didn't seem to like it one bit.

"I understand," he said, "you want to file on this particular section. But you are not old enough to file—you are only nineteen."

"How does it happen," I asked, "that everybody who knows George Dupre in this town seems to know my exact age?"

"Now lookee here, you bald-headed eagle," Mike said, crowding close, "none of that stuff. Hell, we've had about enough of this bedamned stalling around. Make out them papers, or whatever you do around here to deserve being left alive, or . . ."

"Stand aside, Mike," Rose Shagnasty said, sweeping him out of her path as she might brush away a fly. She leaned far over Engle's desk, her huge bosom thrust practically under his startled nose. "I don't know exactly what's going on here but I'm beginning to smell a rat. First the lad can't get a marrying license, even though he needs one bad, and now you start stalling—are you one of George Dupre's stooges too?"

"I'll have you know," Engle said indignantly, "that I represent the United States Government."

"No wonder you're stalling then." Rose sighed. "All you government slobs does that."

"Engle," I said, moving up, "I know that I'm not yet twenty-one. But I was married not five minutes ago to this lady right here—Joan Bauer—in Judge Stark's chambers. And that, Mr. Engle, makes me the head of a family, and as the legal head of a family I am entitled to file on land, even if I was still wearing diapers. So, damn it, man, I'm filing, and if you don't file me I'm going down to the depot and wire Washington about it."

"Hell," Mike said. "Hear the boy talking—sounds off just like his Pa."

Engle, if he was stalling, didn't stall anymore. He made out the filing papers and I signed them. There was a moment of embarrassment when I didn't have enough money to pay the filing fee, but Mike pulled out a roll that would choke a cow and paid it. When I told him that I would pay him back he said, "Forget it. The show was worth it. Hell, what's the hurry anyhow? That girl of yours don't look to me like she is going to calve for months. Still, I guess a feller gets kind of excited when his lady comes around and tells him a thing like that, especially when he ain't expecting it. You wasn't expecting it, was you?"

"Damn you, Mike," I said. "Help me find Fillbuster. Jed Dupre and Steve Holden are holding Pa and Uncle Pete, and Shagnasty, down in the old Box Gulch ranch buildings that I just filed on."

"Now he tells us," Rose Shagnasty said.

"He's been trying to tell you," Joan cried out, "for the past half hour. But you wouldn't listen. And you had better listen now, because I'm only going to say this once. Tom and I did not have to get married—not the way you mean. We got married so Tom could file on land, and we've been engaged for some time and were going to get married anyway when he got back from the south. Tom had to race one of George Dupre's hands into town and get here ahead of him, because he was going to file on the land we wanted, for George Dupre, and if you all don't help us find Sheriff Fillbuster I'm going to get mad and . . ."

Right then Fillbuster came up the stairs with Dennis and down the hall, where we were just coming out of the land-office door, and I was never happier to see anyone in my life.

CHAPTER TEN

Matt Fillbuster, county sheriff, was a man to inspire confidence. Tall, broad-shouldered, a one-time cattleman, lean-hipped, middle-aged, with calm, gray eyes, and a way of looking at a man when you spoke to him that told you that he was listening and evaluating what you were saying.

"What's going on here, Tom?" he asked as we walked toward the door and started down the courthouse steps.

"He's been shot," Ma said. "Look at his back, Sheriff."

Fillbuster looked.

"Superficial wound," he said. "Looks like a bullet. How did it happen, Tom?"

"Jed Dupre shot me," I said. "He and Steve Holden and a man named Jack Stockman jumped us when we were camped in the old Box Gulch ranch buildings. I managed to get away and beat Stockman here."

"Beat him here?" Fillbuster queried.

"Yes," I said. "Jed was just trying to get back at us for sending him to jail, but Stockman was evidently hired by George Dupre to file on the land for him to get later."

"Where are the others?"

"When I jumped Jed, and got away, Jed and Steve were tying them up. They stampeded our horses, but Filly hung around, and I rode her in bareback—there she is out there now. Take care of her, will you, Mike?"

"I see," Fillbuster said. "Well, I'll get my deputy and ride out there and look into this. Seems like six months in the pen didn't do Jed and Steve much good. Now you better get over to Doc Foster's office and have that back looked to. So, Jed shot you, did he—we'll see about that."

"I'll be riding south with you, Sheriff," I said.

"No!" Ma and Joan cried out in unison. "You can't let him, Sheriff. He rode all night with that back not cared for."

That's the way it was when Jack Stockman joined us. He came trudging down the street without his hat and his yellow hair standing on end, his eyes latched on to me and one side of his jaw so swollen that the swelling had blacked and closed his left eye.

"So," he said to Fillbuster, "you got him, did you."

"What do you mean by that?"

"Why, this hairpin attacked me when I was camped out of town a ways and knocked me cold with the barrel of his .45, and then stole my horse and left me afoot."

"You don't say. Tom, what do you have to say about this?"

"I hit him," I said, "with my fist, not with a .45. I have never carried one in my life—you know that, Fillbuster."

"But you did hit him, and steal his horse."

"No. I merely took his horse to town and then turned it loose with everything he owned still on it."

"That," Fillbuster said sternly, "is against the law."

"Against the law," I snapped. "Now, look here, Fillbuster, this man was with Jed and Steve when they held us up, and he threw a gun on us, just like they did. And Jed sent him in to beat us to filing on the land and Jed admitted that he was filing on it for George Dupre. I had every right to stop him."

"If you can prove that," Fillbuster said, "that is a conspiracy between George Dupre and this man. This thing is getting pretty complicated. We'd better go back in and see the judge."

So we all surged back into Judge Stark's chambers, and with us were the two drunks, Ross Shultz and Peter

O'Brian. The judge seemed somewhat startled to see us all back again.

"What's this all about now, Fillbuster?"

Mike didn't give him time to answer.

"Hell, Your Honor," he exclaimed. "Damned if I know. Seems like we had a wedding and then this yellow-eyed rattler came tramping into town like a sore-foot lizard—t'ain't decent, Your Honor—a wedding's supposed to be—"

"Shut up, Flaherty," the judge snapped. "Fillbuster?"

"This man claims," Fillbuster said, "that Conway busted him—"

"In der snoot," Shultz put in. "In der beer spitten."

"Well, I'm damned," Judge Stark declared, adjusting his spectacles and peering down at Shultz from his elevated perch. "Shut up, Shultz. Now get on with it, Fillbuster. I must say that this is most unusual."

"It is unusual," Fillbuster said. "You see, I don't know which of these two to toss in jail. Conway admits tackling Stockman here, but he claims that before that Stockman shoved a gun in his face and then took off to Coyote Wells to beat him to filing on some land that they wanted down there."

"So, Conway admits the attack, does he?"

"Yes," I said. "But Stockman was hired by George Dupre to come in and beat my uncle to filing, while George Dupre's son, Jed, and Steve Holden held my uncle and my pa and Shagnasty Smith prisoners in the old Box Gulch ranch buildings. I caught up with Stockman and I stopped him long enough for me to get in here and file on the land myself."

"If," Judge Stark said, "you can prove that Stockman here and George Dupre were in conspiracy, they'll have to suffer the consequences. As far as your attack on Stockman is concerned, it seems to me to boil down to a matter of intent. If you attacked him merely to prevent him, as a private citizen, from beating you to this courthouse, you are guilty as hell. But, on the other hand, if you had concrete evidence, which you can prove, mind you, that he was acting as a conspirator with George Dupre, to prevent you from filing, you were, perhaps, justified in your action against him. This is something that will have to be threshed out in court. I advise you both to obtain counsel to defend you and appear here—let me see now what I have coming up. Oh, yes, both of you be here at ten sharp on Friday morning."

"I may not be able to have my witnesses here by then," I said.

"In that case you may ask for a delay of trial. If it seems necessary the court will grant it."

"Never heard so many tall words in my life," Mike said.

"What in hell," Fillbuster asked, "will I do with these two between now and Friday?"

Stark leaned over his bench and thrust his jaw out and glared down at Fillbuster.

"I don't give a hoot in the hot place," he declared, "what you do with them; just see that they appear here at the appointed time. Now clear this place, Fillbuster, and throw those two drunks in the clink to sober up. Put them both in the same cage so they can kill each other, and good riddance."

We all filed out of the courtroom again and as we were going down the steps we met George Dupre coming up, his dark, cold snake eyes in sharp contrast to his gray sideburns and immaculate clothing. He laid a detaining hand on Fillbuster's arm.

"What's going on here, Fillbuster?"

Fillbuster shook the hand from his arm.

"It seems," he said, "that your son, Jed, is on the loose again. Held up the Conway party down south. Do you know this man here, Jack Stockman?"

"Distant cousin of mine," Dupre said. "Why? What's he done?"

"Tom Conway here claims that he was hired by you to file on the old Box Gulch ranch section for you, mainly to keep his uncle from getting it."

"That," Dupre said, letting his cruel eyes rest on me, "is a lie, but what I expect from a Conway."

"Hell, Fillbuster," Mike declared, "I never knowed of Tom doing any lying, but this here Dupre character lies every time he breathes."

"Take your hand off of my arm, Dupre," Fillbuster said. "Tom, you get over and see Doc Foster. Stockman, see to it that you appear before Judge Stark on Friday. I'll be riding south with my deputy in about an hour."

"I'll be riding with you," I said.

"No!" Joan cried out. "Your back . . ."

"He's been riding all night with that wound in his back, Sheriff," Ma said.

"If," Fillbuster said as he turned away, "you have that back properly cared for and grab off a wink or two of sleep before I leave, you can go along; otherwise—Shultz, O'Brian, come with me."

"I'll be going along," I said grimly. "Mike, will you put Filly up in the livery and see that she is fed and curried and rubbed down, and hire me a good mount and tie it in front of Doc Foster's office. Come on, Ma. Dennis, how about going along with us—I may need you."

I reached out and gathered Joan in, my arm around her slim waist.

"Good Lord," I said, "are you really my wife—you're beautiful!"

"Tom, not here. Not now. The doctor . . ."

We headed for the doctor's office as Mike went off with Filly. The doctor cleaned and dressed my wound, which proved to be a short gash, almost a bullet burn, fired so close to me that powder had burned the cloth of my shirt and powder grains were embedded in my flesh.

"Lucky," Doc said, "that the bullet missed the spine. It

just went through the roll of flesh behind your left shoulder. If you don't get infection in it you'll have a nice scar to prove that you been to war."

"Doc," I said, "have you got a room with a couch or something in it where I can lay down and take a nap for a few minutes? You have?"

"Capital!" Dennis said.

"Dennis," I said, "you and Mike see to it that I'm called when Fillbuster gets ready to leave, will you?"

Dennis nodded and went out as Doc ushered me into a tiny room with a white-sheeted cot in it. Boots and all, I went down and stretched out.

"We'll have a honeymoon," I said to Joan, and she smiled and put a finger to my lips.

"I know, Tom," she said. "Now you must sleep. . . ."

I didn't hear any more because that seventy-five miles of riding blew up in my face in a flash of darkness, and I slept. I was awakened by somebody shaking my shoulder and when I opened my eyes I was looking up into Joan's eyes, so I just reached up and pulled her down on my chest and we were that way when Mike barged in, saw what was going on, and tried to back out and knocked over some of Doc's medical equipment.

"Hell," he apologized, "the three of them ganged up on me."

"What do you mean?" I demanded to know. "Who ganged up on you—you mean to tell me Jed's in town?"

"Hell no. I mean Joan here and Rose and your ma— insisted I let you sleep for three hours."

"Three hours," I crowed, coming off the bunk in a hurry. "That means that Fillbuster is gone. Let me out of here. When did he leave?"

"About two hours back," Mike said, "but I got a horse waiting for you out here that will make the difference."

I was on that horse and galloping down the street in one minute flat. As the animal beneath me began to stretch out in its stride I knew that I had some real horse flesh under me and wondered where Mike had gotten it. He didn't own a horse that could cover the ground like this one was, and this was no for-rent livery horse. Somewhere Mike had managed to pick up a horse better than any he owned, and better than the livery could offer, a rangy, fleet-footed, dappled gray that really knew how to pick them up and lay them down.

I knew how Fillbuster traveled, slow and steady and sure, right to the end of the trail. He wouldn't be traveling as fast as I was, and I hoped to be able to overtake him by the time he reached the Elk. I felt a fondness for Mike then, and looked back over the years to the day when I'd first met him, when we had just arrived from Massachusetts, and he came toward us with a quarter of beef over his shoulder and the gorgeous Montana sunset flaming behind him. And I thought of all the things he had done for us since then—the biggest-hearted Irishman in the world. And now, in some way, he had found this magnificent horse for me to ride. My back hurt, but it was a clean, well-bandaged sort of hurt and, I hoped, not the hurt of infection. As I rode I ate sandwiches and drank water from a flask that somebody—probably Joan and Ma—had provided. With food and three hours of sleep I felt fine, particularly when I noticed that there was a Winchester carbine in the saddle scabbard. I reckoned that I might need it before this ride was over.

It was two o'clock when I left Coyote Wells and seven o'clock when I caught Fillbuster and his deputy, Hank Boomer, watering and resting their horses at the Elk. Boomer, a slim, quick-moving man of about thirty years, met me as I came down from my horse, and I saw Fillbuster rise up from a small fire with a coffeepot in his hands.

"I see you made it," he said. "That's a good horse you've got there."

"How'd you know it was a good one?"

"Know the horse. Belongs to Breckenridge. See the

brand there, Walking B Bar. Breckenridge must have been in town—that's his personal mount."

"Maybe," I said, "Breckenridge don't like the Dupres."

"Or," Fillbuster commented as he poured me a tin cup of coffee, "he likes the Conways."

I drank the coffee as I led the horse to drink at the Elk, loosened the cinches, and raised the saddle blanket to let air in to the sweaty back of the gray.

"Better pull that saddle," Fillbuster said, "and put it on Segundo—he's picketed over there on my throw rope."

"Segundo!"

"Yeah," Fillbuster said. "As we come south we ran into Segundo, and that big red hoss of Bill Bullow's, headed north. Then, a little later, we picked up a bay mare carrying your brand. No saddles."

"Lady Bird," I said, "headed for their home ranges. The saddles should be at the Box Gulch—that is, if Jed and Steve haven't set fire to them or something."

"He wouldn't do that," Deputy Boomer said. "That would be crazy."

"Jed," I said, "acts like he is crazy—crazy with hate and self-importance. His father brought him up to think that he was the kingpin of the herd and that he could push against the world and it would back off and get down on its knees. When he got sent to jail it left him so full of hate that you can see it in his eyes. I wouldn't put anything past him."

"Eat a bite," Fillbuster said, "and we'll shove on. Those three fresh horses give us the edge."

"I've eaten. The women gave me some sandwiches."

We rode out, mounted now on Segundo, Lady Bird, and Big Red, and leading the others. Three hours out of the Elk we ran into Pa and Uncle Pete and Shagnasty. They saw our horses outlined against the stars on a rise and hailed us, and I recognized Pa's voice.

"You all right, Pa?" I called into the darkness.

"A little bruised," Pa called back. "Who's with you, son?"

"Fillbuster and his deputy, Boomer."

"Good," Pa called back as they approached.

And so we met, and dismounted, and stood there together in the starlit darkness of the Montana night, talking about what had happened since I had bolted out the door with Dupre's carbine bellowing over my back and Steve Holden staggering aside from the thrust of my shoulder. As we stood there a match flared as Pa lit his pipe, and the horses were disturbed by the sudden light and I heard them moving about and the creak of saddle leather and the howling of a coyote on the ridge.

"When you dove out the door, son," Pa said, "I yelled at Jed to let you go because you were too young to file on land. But he turned and shot anyway, but we knew that he missed because we could hear your boots pounding as you ran, apparently unhurt. Shagnasty would have tackled them but I held him back."

"Let me go," Shagnasty grunted, "and I grab and clap heads together—crack like nuts."

"You'd have been shot," Pa said, "either by Steve or Jed. That Jed's fast as greased lightning. He acts to me, Fillbuster, like a real killer."

"I was outside," I said, "wondering if I should go back and try to help you or head for Coyote Wells to get Fillbuster. I decided that you were all right, because only two shots had been fired and both of them at me. I figured that they still had you pinned down."

"They did," Uncle Pete said. "I was scared stiff, staring down those two gun barrels."

"How'd you get away?" Fillbuster asked.

"Shagnasty," Pa said, "hooked a foot under one of those benches at the table and hoisted it clean across the room at Jed. The thing had a two-inch-thick plank top. Jed fired, all right, but just like Shagnasty thought, the bullet hit the bench and was deflected. Went right through, though; you don't stop a 30–30 slug that easy. Shagnasty dove for Jed, right behind the flying bench, and clouted him clear across the room. He lit on top of our saddles and gear in the corner. Steve seemed to be going to shoot at Shagnasty so Uncle Pete here tackled him like a tiger. I grabbed up the bench and slapped Steve in the face with it, knocking him down. I thought that we had them on the hip then. I dove for Steve's gun, which he'd dropped, but he beat me to it. When I saw it in his hands, and Jed sitting on our gear, jacking a cartridge into his saddle carbine, I quit and held up my hands and yelled at Shagnasty to quit too."

"I never took mine down," Uncle Pete said. "I never tackled Steve like no tiger, like you said. I just sort of collapsed on him. Reminds me of the time—"

"Never mind," Pa cut in, "what it reminds you of. Anyway, we backed off from those guns and Jed was like to be tied, so mad that he had spittle foam at his lips. I think that Steve would have pistol whipped us but Jed just motioned to the door with his rifle barrel and told us to get out and start walking, and we did."

"He couldn't do anything else," Fillbuster said. "He knew that Tom was free outside, but he didn't know that he had a horse. He knew that you older folks couldn't walk it to town in two days, but he thought that a youngster like Tom might make it in one, and bring me back in a hurry. You couldn't do him any harm on the loose without weapons, but you could do him a lot of harm if he was foolish enough to stay there, holding you, until Tom brought me back. Jed may have been frothing at the mouth but he was still using his head."

"What do we do now?" Pa asked.

"If it wasn't for your saddles and gear being at the Box Gulch ranch buildings," Fillbuster said, "I'd stay right where we are until daylight. Then I'd head west and try to cut the trail Jed and Steve will make as Jed swings wide of this trace to avoid meeting us and heads out north, where he can get in touch with his father. George Dupre has always backed him in any devilment he got into, and Jed will be looking for cover from his father, wanting to get where George can protect him. He'll either head for Medicine Hills or Antelope Flats. George has ranch interests at both places and is thicker'n thieves with the mayors of both towns, Hi Slocum and Silas Witherspoon."

"Antelope Flats!" I exclaimed. "That's where Witherspoon has his dry-goods store and saloon. The place is the headquarters for every character on the loose in the country."

"Probably," Fillbuster said dryly, his weathered features illuminated as he fired his pipe, "but we haven't been able to prove it so far. You know that we tried to tie Witherspoon in with the men who rustled your cattle, along with Jed and Steve, but weren't able to do it. That lawyer that George brought down from Miles City to defend Steve also defended Witherspoon."

"Well," Uncle Pete said sadly, "they got what they were after. They stopped us from filing on the Box Gulch section and their man, Jack Stockman, had plenty of time to beat Tom to town."

"He didn't beat me into town, Uncle Pete," I said. "Filly wouldn't leave me. She didn't stray and came to me as soon as I got clear of the buildings. I rode her bareback and hit Coyote Wells a half hour ahead of Stockman."

"You did!" Pa exclaimed. "Good boy. A pity you were too young to file."

"I was too young," I said, "but I filed anyway."

"That," Pa said firmly, and I could imagine him clamping down hard on his pipe stem, "is agen the law. It won't stand up in court."

"It will," I said, "because I stood up in court with Joan Bauer and married her."

"Married her! You ain't old enough for that neither. And

do you mean to stand there and tell me that while we were sitting out here under Jed's guns like ducks in a mud puddle, you were lally-gagging around in town, courting a girl and then leading her to the altar. We could have been killed. . . ."

"I sent for Fillbuster," I said, "the minute I hit town, and I didn't think a few minutes, one way or the other, would make much difference with you at the Box Gulch. So while Dennis Flaherty was going after Fillbuster I took time to file on the land."

"You couldn't," Pa declared. "You're too young—Gad, I see it now, you married the girl and got to be the head of a family. Gad, didn't the woman sort of back off there—I couldn't have charged up and ran Ma to the preacher that way. There was this feller with the waxed mustache and . . ."

"I know," I said, "the squint. Actually, the whole deal didn't take more than thirty minutes. You see, Ma was there and the Flaherty brothers were there, and Rose Shagnasty. And Mike Flaherty grabbed the county clerk by the shirt front and lifted him clean off the floor. Judge Stark was kind of mad, too, because O'Brian had bashed Shultz in the nose, I mean snoot, and spit in his beer, but Shultz claimed that O'Brian had spit in his beer first and . . ."

"What in hell," Pa yelled, "are you talking about? I've been shot at and walked fifteen miles and my feet are wore down to the ankles and you stand there talking about folks spitting in each other's beers."

"Balderdash!" Uncle Pete put in. "Forget the bedamned beer, John. Did you say that you managed to file on that land?"

"Yes," I said. "Sorry, Uncle Pete, but it was either me, or Stockman getting it for the Dupres."

"Don't worry about it. I was feeling rather sneaky about filing on it anyway, considering that you located it and wanted it. I'll get me some land on that brook, above or below yours."

"Creek," Pa said, "not brook. If you ain't the lucky one, boy. You file on the best land in the country and marry the prettiest girl in the country, just like that, just like snapping your fingers."

"I wouldn't say that," Fillbuster said. "All the kid did was tackle Jed, get shot in the back, ride bareback fifty miles, knock Jack Stockman cold five miles out of town, and face down the girl and everybody in the courthouse. I'd hardly call that snapping the fingers."

"Shot in the back!" Pa said. "I saw that shot hit the floor. I never knew it touched you. How bad is it, son?"

"Just a scratch, and Doc Foster took care of it in town."

"Well, I'm a short-horned heifer," Pa's voice sounded stunned in the darkness of the night, "if the danged kid ain't growed up. I couldn't have done better myself."

"You," Uncle Pete declared, "couldn't have done half as well, and you darned well know it."

"For once," Pa said, "I'll agree with you, Pete. But don't expect to get in the habit. Well, Fillbuster, what do we do now?"

"We head," Fillbuster said, "for the Box Gulch ranch buildings as fast as these tired horses can take us, so that we can find out what the situation is there. If Jed and Steve are there, and you are prepared to bring action against them, I'll charge them with attempted murder and bring them back to Coyote Wells. If they aren't there, me and my deputy will get on their trail and bring them in."

"I hope," Uncle Pete complained, "that they ain't stole the saddles. Riding bareback ain't my idea of top sport."

"Maybe," Pa said sarcastically, "we can find an old harness there at the Box Gulch. Then you could feel right at home again, with a pair of harness hames to hang on to."

Whatever Uncle Pete might have retorted in reply to that crack of Pa's was cut short by Fillbuster's command.

"Mount up," he said, "and let's get on with it. After I look things over at Box Gulch I may have to deputize you fellows as my posse."

"Deputize!" Uncle Pete exclaimed. "Wait until I write folks back East about this—me a deputy sheriff, chasing outlaws around out West."

CHAPTER ELEVEN

And as we rode on toward the Box Gulch I mulled over in my mind about being deputized and helping Fillbuster run Jed and Steve down. With a charge of attempted murder against them, which shooting a hole in my back and shooting at Shagnasty made quite possible, Jed, with his father behind him, would be hard to find and dangerous to corner. He'd had one dose of imprisonment and I felt that he would do anything, even murder, to see that he didn't wind up there for years. But it wasn't the murder charge that bothered me.

Jed had challenged me and had helped steal our heifer. I had helped trail him down and witnessed against him in court. But down inside I knew that I was not a violent or vindictive man, and neither was Pa. Jed and Steve and Stockman had conspired against us to try to see that we didn't get the Box Gulch land, and we had taken counter-measures and defeated them. And that was enough. I had no desire for revenge, for pursuit. I only had the desire, a gnawing hunger, to turn back north, to Joan, to start with her a new life, to make plans to fix up the Box Gulch buildings for the coming winter, to get in fuel and food, and to trail some of our stock down there to relieve the pressure on the homestead range and on Pa, who would be without my help once I moved south with Joan. I wanted to fill those chinks between the logs, to put panes of glass in the windows, to do something to the fallen-in barn so that Filly and whatever other horses I had would have winter shelter. And above all I wanted Joan, my wife. I wanted to stand by her side, with smoke coming out of our chimney, and Filly by my side, and look out over the Box Gulch stream, across the meadowland to the hills beyond. It had all started as a dream and some of the dream had come true on this day, but most of the dream lay ahead, and I wanted to get on with it, not chase after men who had tried to bring me down and had failed. Perhaps Fillbuster was reading my thoughts as he rode beside me.

"Jed and his father," he said, "tried to stop you here, Tom. Keep a sharp eye out, because they ain't ones to quit easy. They're apt to try again."

When they try again, I thought, that will be time enough to turn on them. Right now I'm sick of it all. Joan's waiting for me in Coyote Wells and that is all that matters now. But we rode on, on the rises where the air was warm and balmy and down into the gullies where the air turned many degrees cooler. Riding fresh horses, we should have hit the Box Gulch by two o'clock in the morning, but three of us riding bareback, and two not used to it, made it slow going. We did not arrive at the little valley of the Box Gulch until just before daylight. The buildings were dark blots on the ground, while beyond, steamy mist drifted over the stream where a flock of mallards rose in panic, with loud complainings. Beyond, in the meadow, a mule deer raised its head and looked and then bounded away, pursued by several others. This flying and bounding disturbed some antelope, fully a half mile away. They flashed their white rumps in the danger signal and then turned and looked to see what it was really all about. It was a wild and a lovely scene and it stirred me. Shagnasty must have felt the same way, for he raised up on his bareback mount and said, "Waugh!" and looked about with one hand above his eyes as though using it to see farther and better.

"Boomer and I'll ride down," Fillbuster said, "and you others split up and surround the place. If they're there and try to make a break for it, get behind a tree or something and yell for them to halt. You have no guns, except for that carbine on the Breckenridge gray, but I don't want any killing—understand?"

"We understand," Pa said.

"Let's go then, Boomer."

They rode down as we began to pull away from each other, to scatter around the rim of the buttes overlooking the buildings. I watched Fillbuster and Boomer ride up to the door and unload and ground tie their mounts at the hitching rail which still was there. I saw them sidle forward, ready for action, and then burst through the door in long strides. And then there were minutes of silence until Boomer appeared and called out to us.

"Come on down—nobody here."

When I entered the room from which I had fled such a short time ago I could see the results of the fight that had taken place there. A long bullet gouge was in the floor where the slug that had creased my back had struck and slithered along until its power was spent. Both benches that had been at the table were now on their sides, and there was a bullet hole through the top of one, with splinters lacing out from where it had emerged. Our saddles and all our pack gear was still there in one corner of the room, and as far as I could see had not been tampered with in any way.

"Don't look like they took anything," I said.

"Couldn't carry much," Pa said, "on their saddle horses. The darned idiots should have hung on to our pack horses."

"Jed," Fillbuster said, "is a dangerous man when cornered, but when he ain't cornered he's a smart man, crafty as a cat."

"Everything here." Shagnasty grunted as he examined the packs.

"They wouldn't need any extra grub," Fillbuster said, "because Jed undoubtedly plans to head for Medicine Hills or Antelope Flats, where he can get in touch with his father.

He'll swing wide of the trace we came in on, so as not to
risk running into us as we come in, and cut a bit west for
Medicine Hills."

Fillbuster stood there, lighting his pipe, apparently deep
in thought as he looked around the room.

"Well, boys," he said finally, "make yourselves at home.
We're going to be here until morning. Picket the horses out
and get some grub and sleep under your belts."

"Should we put out a guard tonight?" I asked.

"No need of it," Fillbuster said. "By now Jed is over at
Medicine Hills or Antelope Flats, beating his gums to some
of his father's hands about how badly he had been treated,
and sending a man off to Coyote Wells to get his father's
help."

"Or," Uncle Pete said grimly, "boasting about how he
cleaned up on us. He looks like the boasting kind to me.
Reminds me of the time the feller kept boasting about how
well fixed he was until finally a lady married him and he
didn't have enough money to pay the preacher. When she
cornered him on it he said, 'Well, I guess I did sort of hide
the facts a bit!' Well, the lady come right back at him and
said, 'Well, as to that, so did I, you see I've got eight kids
that I didn't tell you about.' And that reminds me of the
time when . . ."

"Aw, dry up, Pete," Pa said as he unrolled his bedroll,
"and let a man sleep."

But I didn't want to sleep. Not right then. I wanted to go
out and get the horses picketed and watered and then I
wanted to walk around on that one square mile of ground
that the government had said I could own if I was man
enough to come down here and live on it for three years.
Me and the government and Joan had a deal and I was
right anxious to get started in on it.

A square mile of land is a lot of ground, especially if it
lies in the middle of an unfenced wilderness. Most riders
don't like walking, and cowboy boots are not very good for

it, but I had always liked to walk, particularly when hunting or trapping, because only on foot could a person closely study the ground. So now I started walking around my section of land. I knew, from the map I'd seen in Coyote Wells, with the buildings drawn in, just about where the lines lay, even though we had not yet located the corners. I estimated that the spring Uncle Pete and I had seen was on the section and went to it now to squat and examine the animal tracks there. The cougar had been there the night before, as had been deer and antelope, coyote and perhaps a mink. The manlike print of a coon showed in the mud. Beyond the meadow, on the east side, the land swelled up gradually to the hills beyond, giving good drainage down toward the Box Gulch, but in their swellings the hills held several coulees, or gulches, which led back into their depths. I walked into the largest of these and grouse whirred up from a thick clump of buffalo berry bushes, their silvery leaves in sharp contrast with the leaves of wild plum. Stunted cedar grew aslant on the steep gulch sides and tiny trickles of water issued here and there which, I knew, would dry when June faded into July and August. Back farther in the gulch I jumped the deer that had been on the meadow that morning and they bounded away and managed to lose themselves in their mysterious manner, leaving a person wondering where they went to. I went back to the Box Gulch and crossed it at a shallow point, where the water still boiled about my knees as I waded it, with my boots carried in my hands.

I had just reached the other side when I heard Uncle Pete yell like he was being attacked by a cougar and jacked a cartridge into the Winchester and bounded toward the sharp bend in the stream which concealed him. I slid to a halt with a grin on my face when I saw the little man chasing a fish that was leaping around on the grass. The sight was particularly amusing because the fish, for all its lively jumping, was only about six inches long.

"You really got a big one there, Uncle Pete," I said, using sarcasm that didn't seem to get through to him.

"Ain't it though," he said excitedly, holding up the prize for me to see. "The brook's lousy with them—I got at least a dozen already."

This fish, which abounded in the Box Gulch, was about six to eight inches long, and completely silver in color, with very large eyes and a flat body. I've never seen it anyplace else, though it must be in other waters. Fishermen later have told me that it had the appearance of a white crappie except it did not have the bars on its body, and a man I met from eastern Oklahoma told me it closely resembled a fish known as the "flier crappie." Anyway, it was some sort of sunfish and very good eating if one had the patience to scale it and clean it, after which there was not very much meat remaining. But with these, and a fairly good-sized catfish Uncle Pete darn near had hysterics over, we had fish for supper that night.

After I managed to pry Uncle Pete away from his fishing, as the sun lowered in the west, we tried to figure out about where my north and my south line would lie. From here we could see just about what kind of land Pete might file on. This far from the railroad there were no railroad sections, so government sections joined government sections, without railroad sections being thrown in between, as they were nearer the railroad, where we had homesteaded.

"It appears," Uncle Pete said as we looked over the land to the south and north, "that any meadow I get against the brook will be long and narrow, not shove out wide to the hills like your meadow does."

"Yes," I said, "but in moving down here, Uncle Pete, you've got to change your way of thinking, from hay and milk cows to beef cattle. True, you want hay land, but buffalo grass grows on those hills, which can be cut for hay, and the land to the south or to the north, considering that you'll have a half mile, the way I figure it, on the creek on

the north section and fully three quarters of a mile on the
creek to the south section, you'll have all the bottom land
you can handle."

"Yeah," Uncle Pete said, flexing his fingers, "I guess I've
been milking cows for so long my mind runs to milk-pail
music and the price of cream."

"Let it keep running there some," I told him, "because
this cattle ranch is going to have a milk cow or two and
milk, butter, cream, and even eggs. I'm going to bring down
a few chickens. Lordy, I wish Fillbuster would forget deputizing us and chasing after Jed and Steve—I want to get on
with my own business."

"Which includes," Uncle Pete cackled, and his quizzical
look, with one rusty-colored eyebrow hoisted higher than
the other and his sly grin, merry eyes, and hat down over
his ears, made him look like a teasing elf, "getting back to a
wife you ain't broke to bridle yet."

"Of course," I said, and felt my face reddening, "I want
to get back to her—ain't hardly seen her since the wedding."

When we got back to the buildings we could see smoke
issuing from the chimney where the cookstove was and
knew that Shagnasty was busy. Pa was sleeping but rolled
around and sat up when Uncle Pete began waving his fish
around and talking loudly of how he caught them.

"I flung my hook out there and the thing had hardly lit
when I got one hell of a yank and—"

"A yank!" Pa exploded, sitting up and eyeing the little
silver fish. "From those things? Are they actual fish, or just
grasshoppers you kicked up out'n the grass?"

"Just jealous," Uncle Pete declared, whipping the catfish
he'd been holding behind his back around and under Pa's
startled nose. "And what do you think of this one, you old
fraud."

"Huh!" Pa said, and his eyes became wary. "Well, that's
better, but it don't hold a candle to the ones I flung
out. . . . What do you mean by fraud?"

"Fraud is what I said and what I meant," Uncle Pete declared. "Back at Coyote Wells you told me that the catfish you caught here were little ones—didn't amount to much—and now you tell me that they were bigger than this one. Seems like I got you sort of backed into a corner. . . ."

"Backed into a corner, my eye," Pa declared. "Anytime you can back this hoss in a corner . . ."

"Too damn much talk," Shagnasty said. "Somebody get wood, and, little man, you better clean fish if we eat now."

When Uncle Pete and I went out to go down to the stream to clean the fish we saw Fillbuster and Boomer standing together to the west, apparently with their heads together talking.

"I wonder," Uncle Pete said, "what the two lawmen are cooking up out there to bring down on us tomorrow. I thought it would be grand to be a deputy sheriff, galloping around, chasing outlaws, but right now I'd settle for a few days away from that saddle."

We found out what they were cooking up after we had eaten and Fillbuster had filled his pipe and leaned back.

"I've changed my mind," he said, "about deputizing you fellows and taking you along after Jed and Steve. The fact that they didn't take anything whatever from your packs shows that Jed is running right back to Papa, as fast as he can make it. There ain't any danger of him forting up in the hills, so I won't need a posse to rout him out. I been thinking about it and it occurs to me that since you, John, didn't know that bullet hit Tom at all, maybe Jed don't know it either. He was aroused and excited, with Tom diving at his legs, and when he fired, looking down that rifle barrel, what he saw the most was that slug hitting the floor and gouging along, throwing up splinters. He probably thought he missed Tom entirely."

"I see," Pa said. "What are you trying to get at, Fillbuster?"

"Well, if he thinks that he didn't hit Tom at all, he may be going to get to his father and try to bluff it out. After all, he can swear that he and Steve and Stockman—or maybe he can swear that Stockman wasn't even with them—were here first and you came in and attacked them and they only defended themselves."

"Why would we attack them?" Uncle Pete asked.

"You wanted this section of land badly. You hurried down to look it over. But when you got here they were in possession, so you tried to throw them out. As far as Jed may be concerned, since he may think that he didn't hit Tom, he can claim that he just fired in the air to hold you off, or even that he didn't fire at all."

"No judge would believe that," Pa said.

"Maybe not," Fillbuster came back at him, "but it would be your word against theirs, and their word would be backed up by George Dupre's lawyers. Bear that in mind."

"Lawyers!" Pa exclaimed. "I ain't got ary money to hire lawyers. Any lawyering to be done, I'll do it myself."

"That I want to see." Uncle Pete cackled. "That would be worth the whole trip out here from Massachusetts."

"Ha," Pa said. "All a person has to do is get up there and tell the honest truth."

"And," Uncle Pete said, "by the time you get done doing that, them lawyers has twisted you into exactly the same shape as a pretzel."

"Where," I asked Fillbuster, "does that leave us?"

"I don't know where it leaves you, but I know where it leaves me and my deputy. Like I told you, Jed Dupre is a dangerous man when he's mad and has his back against the wall, but when he's free to move he's as crafty as they come. He didn't take a single thing of yours so that he couldn't be stuck with a charge of theft, so I think he's going to try to wiggle through it. But I can't be sure."

"What, then, are you going to do?" I asked.

"Me, I'm going to take my deputy and circle around and

locate the trail he took out of here. Then I'm going to follow it wherever it leads, and take whatever action seems necessary as things develop."

"Hell of a note," Pa grumbled. "They stack up agen us with guns, take a couple of shots at us, and then slip away and leave us in complete confusion."

"I reckon," Uncle Pete said dryly, "that you was born confused. Now I haven't known you since you were borned, mind you, but I've known you since you was about knee high to a short man, and the way I look at it . . ."

"Who gives a hoot about the way you look at it," Pa retorted, and he winked broadly at me.

"Well," Fillbuster said, "let's get to bed and get some sleep. In the morning I'll head out on their trail and you folks better head back for Coyote Wells. But keep your eyes open on the way."

"Sleep," Uncle Pete said. "That suits me to a fair-you-well."

"Me too," I said as I picked up my bedroll and went out the door, feeling glad that we'd head for home in the morning, and Joan.

CHAPTER TWELVE

I moved down to the stream and selected a level spot on which to lay my bedroll, which consisted of two blankets and a canvas tarp long enough to go under and over the blankets. Daylight still lingered over the meadow but dark shadows were aslant across the steep, buttelike rises behind and to the north of the buildings. As I sat on my bed, pulling off my boots, I saw the flight of mallard ducks come in, make a circle of the meadow, then curve their wings and extend their red legs as they prepared to lower down to the water. One by one they splashed in, talking to each other like ladies at a tea party, and then seemed to separate into pairs for mating, since this was late spring. The sight stirred me deeply, as the flight of waterfowl always did, whether they be ducks or geese.

Sitting here, thinking about this, my mind went back to the days when I used to slip down to the Sandstone from our one-room homestead shanty, when the eastern sky was barely turning gray, lugging Grandpa Hobson's heavy, lever-actioned Winchester shotgun, to sneak up on the potholes of the creek. Some things a man experiences only once in its fullest, most brimming measure, for although the experience may hold strong flavor for him through life, it can never again equal that first time it touched his life. Sitting here now, watching the mallards swim about before me, I could once again smell the acrid scent of powder as it drifted on the breeze, with Mike Flaherty shouting from where he had toppled from the cut bank into the mud, with

Pa rushing toward me to congratulate me on the two ducks I'd knocked down. That was, no doubt, a part of it, but most of it was that these birds warned us of the coming of winter when they flew south and announced the approach of spring when they returned. We watched them when they left with a feeling of sadness, of being left behind, and greeted them joyously when they returned when the first real chinook wind melted the snow and flooded the basins of the prairie.

A towering bank of clouds was building swiftly now in the northwest; a huge, high-flung, menacing mass swept across the sky, roiled with wind that did not yet touch me where I sat. Thunder rumbled in the black mass as it blotted out the setting sun and darkness came to the meadow swiftly as the cloud shadow raced across the flatland to strike the hills beyond. Jagged flashes of lightning made their fiery arrows and thunder moved across the plain like the rolling wheels of giant chariots. The air was deathly still, and then a cool breeze sprang up from the northwest which held the pungent, wet-prairie scent of rain and electric ozone. Huge drops, widely spaced, began to spatter on my tarp and I slipped into my bedroll and covered my head against them. And then, as swiftly as it came the storm was gone, leaving behind it night's darkness and a glitter of stars, newborn, and all that was left of it was a grumble of thunder to the east, where it had gone, and as this died away the song of the stream once again took over the stillness of the night.

I awakened with dew on my face and a sense of having slept well, feeling strong and fit, except for the soreness beneath the bandage on my back. A thread of smoke was issuing from the chimney at the ranch building so I hastened to pull on my clothes and roll up my bed. Then I washed myself in the ice-cold water of the Box Gulch and went to the house, where Shagnasty and Uncle Pete were busy about the stove and Pa was grumbling in his stockinged feet and shaking out his boots, peering into them as though he expected something to jump out at him. Fillbuster and Boomer were not there.

"Critters," Pa complained, "were galloping around on my bed all night. Now, if I was as small as these damned things, I'd have sense enough to stay away from something a couple hundred times as big as I was. But not these varmints. They was so damned mad last night that I'd hidden my pipe and tobacco that I could hear them gritting their teeth."

"Gritting their teeth," Uncle Pete said. "You couldn't hear no little animal like a mouse grit its teeth, even if they was to do it."

"Little animals." Pa hooted. "The things which was loping around on my tarp had feet like jackrabbits. I could hear them gnashing their teeth. . . ."

"Gnawing hole," Shagnasty said, "in grub box."

"Ha!" Uncle Pete said.

"Well," Pa declared, "what's the difference between grit, gnash, and gnaw? Anyway, I heard them."

"Grit, gnash, gnaw." Uncle Pete looked at me and whirled one finger around his head as though to indicate that Pa was slightly daft.

I left then to take the horses off their picket ropes and bring them to the stream for watering and then to the hitch rail before the house, which leaned a bit but still stood. By the time this was done Shagnasty stuck his homely face out the door and yelled to come and get it. So I went in and sat down to coffee, sour-dough hotcakes, and eggs, which we carried buried in oats against breakage. Fillbuster and Boomer had evidently slept up on the buttes because they came from that direction, carrying their rolled-up beds. The thought came to me that perhaps the sheriff had not been so sure as he had made out that we didn't need a guard out and had slept clear of the buildings as a precaution. The pair of lawmen got out their eating utensils and sat down.

"Good grub, Shagnasty," Fillbuster said, but the big man only grunted in reply. He had a plate over by the stove from which he ate prodigiously, while pouring out the batter for the cakes, which were as light and fluffy as a man could wish. I'm sure that Shagnasty would have chased Jed with murder in his heart if Dupre had stolen his precious pot of aged sour dough. After we were through eating we all began to prepare to leave. The lawmen got away first, and I saw them circle to pick up the trace of Jed's shod horses and then take off to the west.

"We can't take all this duffle along," Pa said, indicating the pile we'd brought on the two pack horses.

"No," I said. "We'll just take bedrolls and grub for two days."

"If we leave the rest," Pa said, "the pack rats and mice will make short work of it."

"Me hang from ceiling," Shagnasty said, looking up at the great center beam which supported the hewn-log rafters. He began sorting out what we'd need and then hung the rest in the packs out of reach of raiders.

Within the hour we were strung out to the south, with bedrolls wrapped in slickers behind our saddles, together with a coffeepot and stew pan and a little grub. We made the Elk Creek camp in daylight and settled down for another evening with the mosquitoes, but the night turned cold early and the pests left. I'd not been much bothered by them on the Box Gulch because the water there ran cold and swift. Later in the season, when it slowed and lowered, we'd probably have more mosquitoes there. But on Montana's high plains the onslaught of mosquitoes is not too long in a land where winter looks over your shoulder even in summer, with early-spring and late-fall nights holding frost. I had found that the mosquitoes bothered the most on flat prairie, where there were many buffalo wallows, made by the huge beasts when they dusted themselves and pawed the ground in mating frenzy. These buffalo wallows held

water from spring's snow melt and were the breeding
grounds for hordes of the bothersome insects. These attacked in the day as well as at night, if the night be warm
enough. At times they gathered in the hollows before Filly's
shoulders, out of the wind, and in such numbers that when I
reached down to sweep them away with my hand my palm
dripped Filly's blood.

After I had checked the horses and settled down in my
bed at the Elk Creek camp, Pa came to squat beside me, oc-
casionally slapping a mosquito, although the night was now
becoming quite chilly.

"So," he said, "you're married."

"Yes."

"Didn't the girl sort of back off when you came galloping
after her and yanked her off to the preacher?"

"Wasn't a preacher. It was Judge Stark."

"All the same," Pa said. "You get married just as solid
with one as with the t'other."

Pa rocked back and forth on his heels for a minute or
two.

"All the same," he said finally, "I'm right glad that you
and the girl came to the house to tell us about it."

"About what?"

"Well, that you planned it and all. Otherwise a person
might get the idea that you married the woman so you
could get the land. Some women might have backed away
from that idea, right smart."

I chuckled.

"Joan did, there for a minute, and I didn't have a minute
to spare. Scared heck out of me, and then she remembered—"

"That you were in love," Pa interrupted.

"I guess that's how it was," I said, embarrassed to be
talking about love with Pa.

"I want you to know, boy," Pa said, "that I appreciate
what you did. Big thing it was. Real big."

"What do you mean?"

"Well," Pa said, "me and your ma got married once. 'Twas a long time ago, forty years or more. But I recall the day right well. Real well. And I don't know if I'd have left Trix right after the preacher said the words and gone riding off for three, four days to see that my pa got out of some fix he was in, like you did. I reckon that I'd probably have left my pa to stew in his own juice until I got around to it."

I sat up in bed.

"You didn't have to ride back here with Fillbuster," Pa said. "You could have let him and his deputy take care of it."

"Of course I had to come along," I said. "How'd I know that you weren't shot or hurt or something and needed me. You're my pa."

"And," Pa said, reaching a big hand out to grip my shoulder, "you're my son. See you come dawn."

And then he went away, a big man any way you looked at him, and I lay back in my bed with a feeling of warmth that the chill of the night could not touch.

We rode out at dawn and came into Coyote Wells with a couple of hours of daylight left. I left the others and hit straight for Prestons', with an eagerness to see Joan that was overwhelming. I ground hitched the big gray horse in the alley and went to the kitchen door and knocked. The door opened and Mrs. Preston stood there with a pan in her hand and a touch of flour on her nose.

"Tom," she said. "You're all right? Joan was worried."

"Joan," I said. "Isn't she here?"

"Of course not," Mrs. Preston said, and then she smiled as she wiped the flour from her nose. "She's out at the ranch with your mother, where she belongs. She's your wife now, Tom."

"Well," I said, using an expression that Pa often used when he was exasperated, "I'll be a short-horned heifer."

"I can hardly," Mrs. Preston said, "imagine you as one of

those, but I do know that you took away the best cook and maid I've ever had and got yourself a better wife than you probably deserve. Now get along—she's waiting for you."

I left there in a hurry and rode straight to the livery stable to get Filly. The stableman told me that Breckenridge had let Mike get the horse for me and left word that it was to be taken care of when I brought it back. Filly blubbered at me with that vibration of her lips that she always greeted me with as I switched my saddle from the gray to her back. And then I was galloping down the street and Filly's hooves were a thunder on the planks of the bridge over the Sandstone at the edge of town. I had expected to shortly overtake the others but when the saged flats of the Bonepile came before me where I could see a mile ahead I realized that they must have stopped off in town, perhaps for a beer or two, though Pa seldom drank. Filly was fresh and eager after her long rest and really stretched out, the breeze blowing her golden mane back over the bulge of the saddle, and I leaned over and talked to her, so glad to have her once again under me that I felt near to bursting with it. A man's life is long, compared to that of a horse, or even a dog, like Rover, and a person knows that, barring accident, that he'll outlive an animal and have his heart wrenched out when the time comes to lose a beast that is, in some circumstances and to some men, as close to him and as dear to him as a member of his family. I had often thought of this in relation to Filly, and to Rover, and the thought gave me a great sadness.

I hauled Filly up in the yard and came down from her, moving swiftly toward the porch, but I hadn't taken a half-dozen steps before the door flew open and Joan came running toward me, and we met there and clung together. I had kissed her many times before, but not like this, long and deep and fully possessing, and when we stepped apart she held me at arm's length, looking me up and down, at my dirty blue shirt, my worn and battered wing chaps, my sweat-stained Stetson, not seeing them, apparently, for all of her looking, for she said, "You look wonderful, my husband."

And then Ma and Rose Shagnasty descended on us and I had my hands full of questions. Where's the others, is Pa all right, is Uncle Pete all right, is Shagnasty all right, did Fillbuster arrest Jed and Steve? And leaping about us, barking, Rover was greeting my fingertips with a wet nose. It was wonderful to be back.

It is amazing how news can spread in a country where folks live miles apart, without telephones, but when a family or a rider goes to town, he collects all the news, and when he goes home he distributes it along the way to anybody he meets or any home he passes, and in some way it spreads until all know. Anyway, the news that we were back and I had married Joan and had filed on the Box Gulch ranch section had gotten around and Mike and Dennis Flaherty and Grandpa and Grandma Hobson and even Bill Bullow dropped around that evening, so I had no more chance to be alone with Joan than a prairie dog in a dog village. As folks talked and gossiped back and forth, the details of my dash into Coyote Wells began to come out, details that neither Pa nor Uncle Pete knew.

"I missed the whole thing," Bill Bullow complained, hunching his huge shoulders forward, his beefy face holding a look of disgust, "damned if I didn't. I was in town later that day and the place was buzzing like a stirred beehive. Women were standing around, chattering like magpies and waving their arms, and most men were leaning up against bars around town, discussing what had happened and hoping that Jed and his bunch would get what they had coming to them. Biggest thing that happened to Coyote Wells since Conway here slapped Silas Witherspoon in the face with a pink cake at the county fair."

I was sitting on the sofa, listening to all this, holding Joan's hand.

"Hell," Mike Flaherty declared, "me and Dennis was smack in the middle of it. I seen Tom come galloping down the street on that strawberry-roan mare of his, without no saddle, and this lady in front of him with no riding skirt on. You could see—hell, pardon me, ma'am."

"Never mind what you could see," Pa said. "Get on with it."

"Well, when I seen them haul up in front of the courthouse and unload and go trotting up the steps like they was in a hell of a hurry, I went over there to see what was up. When I come in they was trying to get Jonas to issue them some sort of a paper and Tom told Dennis to rush off and get Fillbuster. When I seen that that popeyed Bert Jonas wasn't cooperating, you might say, I picked him up by the front of the shirt and sort of shook him."

"Sort of shook him," Pa said.

"Hell yes. The rattler's heels was playing a drumbeat on the front of that there counter. Feller don't weigh more'n hundred and fifty pounds."

"I see," Pa said.

"But he sure writ out that paper fast when I let him down."

"Capital!" Dennis exclaimed.

"Yes," Rose Shagnasty put in, "and I'll never forget the look on Judge Stark's face when Mike bellied up to him and demanded that he marry Tom and Joan, right when he was all flustered up about two drunks spitting in each other's beer."

"This is the second time," Pa said, "that I've heard something about folks spitting in each other's beer . . . what's the story, anyhow?"

"Well, you see," Rose explained, "there were these two drunks, Ross Shultz and Peter O'Brian. O'Brian was so stupefied that he couldn't even focus his eyes. He just stood there, sort of swaying this way and that, owl-eyed, but Shultz was trying to explain to the judge with that German accent of his." And then Rose went into a gale of laughter, her huge bosoms shaking like jelly.

"He said—he said," she finally gasped out, "that this shmaltz vollop me on mine nose—der snoot, und I vollop him und—Himmel—he in my face spitten."

"And then," Mike roared, "when the judge accused him of spitting in O'Brian's beer, he said that he didn't because he missed."

"And all the time Mike here was trying to get rid of the drunks so that the judge would marry Tom and Joan."

Rose went off into gales of laughter again and it caught on and everybody, even Grandpa Hobson, who is usually sober-faced, joined in until the old homestead shack was filled with it, and I put my arm around Joan's slim waist and squeezed a bit, secure in the knowledge that these people, these wonderful friends of mine, were talking and laughing before her in a way that they would not have done if they had not accepted her as one of them. There would be no gradual acceptance or rejection of Joan, I knew, and this made me very proud and happy.

"And then," Rose went on, "when Fillbuster asked the judge what he should do with Tom and Stockman between then and Friday, the judge leaned down from his desk and glared at Fillbuster and told him that he didn't give a hoot in the hot place what he did with them as long as he saw to it that they showed up when he told them to. Lordy, Tom, you have to appear on Friday, and this is Wednesday."

"Yeah," Bill Bullow said, "I heard about that. Have you got a lawyer yet, Tom?"

"Lawyer," Pa said. "What would he need a lawyer for? Stockman and Jed and Steve Holden threw guns down on us and Jed sent Stockman off to file on our land. Tom beat him to it, that's all. I don't need ary lawyer for an open-and-shut case like that. I'll be all the lawyer he'll need."

"I'd think about that for a while," Bill Bullow cautioned.

"If you could prove that George Dupre set this thing up and hired Stockman to file on the place for him to take over later, or just to beat you out of it for pure spite, George would face a conspiracy charge himself, and the judge would throw any suit against Tom out of court. But George ain't going to take any chances on a thing like that. He'll have a high-priced attorney down from Miles City to defend Stockman, because if he don't, Stockman might get his tongue tangled up and admit that Dupre hired him to file on the land, with an agreement to turn it over to Dupre after he proved up on it."

"I don't need ary lawyer," Pa repeated. "All we have to do is tell Judge Stark the straight truth of the matter."

"The straight truth," Bill Bullow said, "has a way of getting all twisted up when a lawyer gets his hands on it."

"That's why we don't want one," Pa said. "I'll be all the lawyer we need."

"That," Uncle Pete cackled, "is something I want to see. It will be worth the trip out here from Massachusetts."

"There's a good chance," Bill Bullow went on, "that there won't be any hearing at all. I wouldn't be surprised if George Dupre don't manage to get Stockman out of the country. If he don't show up, the judge would throw the whole thing out of court. And, of course, a hearing before Judge Stark ain't at all like a judge trying a case in Miles City or Chicago. Stark just lets everybody have their say and asks questions of everybody concerned and then makes up his mind on the deal. If folks don't like his decision they can take it up to a higher authority. It would be all right, John, for you not to have an attorney—that is, if Dupre didn't have one for Stockman, but he will have. An attorney could get you all tangled up in your own rope."

"He's been tangled in his own rope," Uncle Pete chuckled, "ever since I knew him as a kid. Always was a mite peculiar. I recall the time . . ."

"I don't give a tinker's damn," Pa roared, "what you recall. I still think that in the United States of America a person can stand up in court and tell the honest-to-God truth and not be handed a raw deal, and that's just what we intend to do."

"Well," Bullow said, "I doubt that Jack Stockman will show up, but just in case he does, we'd better scatter around tomorrow and gather up a few folks who know you and Tom, to sort of back you up, like a cheering team at a high-school baseball game."

So that's the way it was left when everybody went home. Ma sighed and said, "Well, it's getting late and time we get to bed."

Pa yawned prodigiously and said, "Yeah, I'm beat out. Feel like I could sleep a week."

"Where's Uncle Pete?" I asked, not seeing him there anymore.

"Oh," Ma said casually, "he decided to ride into Coyote Wells for the night. Said something about staying at the hotel."

"Hotel!" I crowed, and then I shut up, realizing that Uncle Pete had cleared out so that Joan and I could have the bedroom together. And then it hit me hard, that I really was married to Joan, and that this was to be only the first night, and that from here on out, for as long as we both lived, this was how it was going to be, just like it had been with Pa and Ma for all these years.

Joan looked at me and blushed and then went into the bedroom and shut the door, while Pa and Ma went into the other bedroom. I sat alone for a minute or two in the kitchen and then went down to the barn, with Rover at my heels, to look to the horses, as I had been in the habit of doing for many years. And then I came back to the house and went to Joan and our marriage at last became real and solid and entirely wonderful.

CHAPTER THIRTEEN

In the morning I sat and watched Ma and Joan working together to get breakfast, and Pa sitting there watching them with happiness in his eyes, and I knew that as far as they were concerned I had chosen the right wife. Ma and Joan were chattering together as they worked and anyone could see that they liked each other.

It was a fine June morning, with the sun making the green carpet of the prairie a thing of beauty, soon to fade as the hot sun of July cured the buffalo grass. Far away, across the saged flats below, I could see wisps of smoke rising from the chimneys of Coyote Wells. A pair of red-tailed hawks were circling in the blue, on the lookout for unwary gophers, and meadowlarks sang from the fence posts. Pa didn't say much during breakfast but I could see that he had something on his mind.

"I reckon," he said as he pushed his chair back, "that we'd best be getting into town and checking up on a few things. We've got to get together with Pete and get our stories straight so that we won't be contradicting each other at the hearing. I don't want to, like Bill Bullow said, get tangled in my own rope."

"All right," I said. "How about you and Ma going to town in the wagon while Joan and I ride in and look over the stock on the way? Mike Flaherty has been keeping an eye on things but I'd like to take a look myself."

"Fine," Pa said. Then, looking at Joan, "You might just as well get used to having a horse under you, because you surely did marry a riding man."

"I like to ride," Joan said. "I'll be ready as soon as I get the breakfast dishes washed. Ma, you go dress—I'll take care of this."

I went to the barn, with Rover chasing at my heels, and saddled Filly and Segundo, rode Filly out into the pasture, and ran in Ned and Spooks and tossed the harnesses on them. I hitched them to the wagon and drove it up before the house. By the time I had this done Joan was ready to go. I helped her into the saddle, proud as a peacock of my pretty wife. She looked down at me from Segundo and gave me that slow, dark-eyed smile and then she said, "Tom, I never thought that I could ever be this happy."

"That makes two of us," I said as I swung up on Filly and checked her urge to go with the reins so that she arched her neck and pranced prettily.

"I must ride her someday," Joan said. "She is the most beautiful animal I've ever seen. And besides, I love her because she brought us together."

"She's a little lively for you to ride yet," I said. "And how did she bring us together?"

"Well," Joan said, "if she hadn't been so beautiful I wouldn't have spoken to you that morning when you came riding by; I'd have let you go by without speaking and you'd never have asked me to go to the dance at the Starvation Flats hall."

"I didn't ask you. I just told you that there was to be a dance and you used it as an excuse to rope me in."

Her joyous laughter that I loved so much tinkled out.

"And never was a man more willing to be roped in."

"I'll agree to that," I said, "but at the time I was scared stiff when I found that in some way I had apparently asked you to go to the dance with me. But after I took you to the dance I made up my mind that I was going to marry you. And now I've went and done it."

"You didn't went and done it," she teased. "I set my cap for you and you couldn't help yourself."

Bantering back and forth, we rode out onto the end of the ridge where we could look down on the Bonepile Creek Flats, and sat there as I had done so many times down through the years, dreaming our dreams now together. With me these dreams had always been of wide, open ranges, with plenty of water, and contented, fat cattle grazing on them, and now it seemed that these dreams might come true, only much better than I had ever dreamed, for now Joan would be a part of them. She completed the perfect picture.

"Down below," I said, "you see a gumbo flat, with stunted sage and cactus, and an alkali creek that only runs when the snow melts in spring, and is at other times a series of bog holes. But the Box Gulch runs the year round, and before our cabin there is a meadow, and around the meadow fertile hills where the grass is still deep and like it was in the days of the Indians and the buffalo. By the time winter sets in a goodly share of our stock will be down there, Joan, and you'll be there with me. It will be a bit rugged, and you could stay here until spring, until I have time to get the place better fixed for a woman."

"You know that I wouldn't do that. Your mother settled here in a one-room shack. I may not be as good a woman as your mother, but I can make a good try to be, Tom."

"I bet you will at that," I said. "Come on, I'll race you to the creek."

And then we were sweeping down off the ridge and riding the two-mile length of the creek to make sure that there were no bogged cattle. I didn't expect to find any because the water was still high enough in the holes that the cattle could reach it without wading in breast-high mud. We rode on into town and when we got there we found Ma in Brannigan's store.

"Your father," she said, "wandered off down the street."

Brannigan looked at me and jerked his head toward his rear storeroom and I followed him there.

"What's on your mind, Sam?"

"That back-East uncle of yours," he told me, "is celebrating your wedding, or something."

"Uncle Pete?"

"Yes. I sent your father off after him, and perhaps you'd better follow him up."

"I see. What's he drinking?"

"Hard apple cider."

"Pa told me that he liked that," I said. "But why worry about it? It won't hurt to let him have a little fling. After all, he had a pretty rough go of it on this trip south."

"The point is," Brannigan said, "that he is doing his drinking in George Dupre's saloon."

"Dupre's saloon! He wouldn't do that—not with the Stockman hearing coming up and all. He could go to Tom Hogan's place for his cider."

"Tom Hogan," Brannigan said, "may not carry prime New York imported cider. And if he does, he didn't send anybody around to tell your uncle about it."

"What do you mean by that?"

"Well, your father, when joking about Pete, never made any secret of the fact that he liked apple cider awfully well. Your uncle was browsing around in here this morning, sober as a judge, when Hank Scofield—you know, he is one of Dupre's bartenders—dropped in and managed to get to talking to Pete. I heard him tell Pete that he was from Massachusetts and then it wasn't but a short time until he'd switched the conversation around to apples and cider. He told Pete that he knew of a place that had the very finest New York hard cider. Pete fell for it, hook, line, and sinker, and off they went, like two chums who had known each other all their lives. That Scofield is sure a slick talker."

"And you smelled a fish," I said.

"You bet I did," Brannigan said. "I waited an hour or more and then slipped over to Dupre's for a beer. Sure enough, your uncle was cozied up at a table with Dupre,

Scofield, and Ollie Lang, another of George's stooges, and Pete was well along toward having a skin full."

I didn't wait to hear any more. If Uncle Pete had gone to Dupre's accidentally, not knowing the town, that was one thing, but being lured there by a Dupre bartender was a different-colored horse. As I stepped out onto the boardwalk I saw Shagnasty riding down the street on Big Red and I stepped out and held up a hand. He pulled up and looked down at me with a slow smile in his black-brown Indian eyes.

"What's up, sprout?" he asked, as lather from Big Red's chomping on the bit sprayed across my sleeve.

When I told him, he remained quiet and thoughtful. When I finished telling him, he swerved Big Red over to Brannigan's hitching rail, came down from the saddle, and in one deft movement slipped the long-barreled 45-70 from the scabbard.

"Dupre." He growled. "Him again. We go take care."

"No, Shagnasty!" I said. "There's no need for guns. As far as I know there's no trouble at all. Now I'm going down to Dupre's place and stroll in casuallike—"

"Me go with," Shagnasty said, reluctantly shoving the big rifle back into the boot.

"No," I said. "That would look like we were looking for trouble. I'll go in and then, in a few minutes, if I don't come out, you come in and order a beer."

"Shagnasty don't drink—everybody know that. I part Cheyenne. I drink I yell and go on warpath—like hell."

"Well then, just come in and stand around."

"All right, sprout. I stand around big."

Big is right, I thought. The mere fact that Shagnasty Smith walked into Dupre's place would in itself be a shock to Dupre. If he came in and just stood there, nigh on to seven feet tall, with his cold, unreadable eyes on George, it just might make the slicker hesitate in whatever he had planned up his oily sleeve.

When I came in through the bat wings Pa was at the bar with a beer in his hand, turned so that he could watch both the bartender and the table where Uncle Pete sat with Scofield, Dupre, and Ollie Lang. Uncle Pete had his back to Pa and did not seem to realize that he was there. Pa gave me a keen glance as I came in and nodded to the bartender, a burly man with his hair parted in the middle and a bushy mustache.

"A beer for my son," Pa said.

"We don't serve minors here," the barkeep snapped.

"So," I said, feeling rising anger, "you know my age, too, do you. Probably got my birth certificate in your pocket."

"Root beer, then," Pa said.

"Ain't got any."

"You're a damned liar," Pa said, and he looked at me and lowered one eyelid in a slow wink. "Let's you and me go over and join the party."

As we walked toward the table together I realized that now I was a bit taller than Pa, a bit heavier, and perhaps wider in the shoulders, and it made me feel real good. If there was to be any trouble over this, I figured that Pa and I, working together, could take care of it. Uncle Pete seemed to sense our approach, for he looked around and saw Pa, and I could see that he was well intoxicated.

"John," he said thickly. "Set down and have a drink. Best bloody apple cider I ever saw—except, of course, that I used to make."

Pa swung a chair around and sat down at the big, green-cloth-topped gaming table, but I stayed on my feet beside him.

"I been hearing some right interesting conversation over at this table," Pa said.

He pointed a work-worn finger at Hank Scofield, a narrow-headed, half-bald, lanky individual with a long, thin nose that had been skidded off to one side, probably by an angry fist.

"For instance," Pa told Uncle Pete, now having gained his owl-eyed attention, "this Scofield character here with the broke nose ain't ever been in Massachusetts. The lousy snake-in-the-grass was born in Antelope Flats, and is Dupre's bartender."

"You don't tell me," Uncle Pete declared, staggering to his feet and wavering like a sheet in the wind. "Then I have been utterly deceived by the gentleman. Utterly deceived."

"You don't say," Pa said.

Uncle Pete drew himself up to his full height.

"I want you gentlemen to know," he declared, "that I am a gentleman from Massachusetts—folks came over on the *Mayflower*. And I don't take kindly to being deceived, Mr. Sco—what did you say your bleeding name was?"

"On the *Mayflower*," Scofield echoed, open-mouthed.

"Certainly," Uncle Pete declared. "Bloody hulk leaked like a sieve. Worked my fingers to the bone, bailing her out. You took a bucket and . . ." Words failed Uncle Pete and he sagged back down in his chair like a pin-pricked balloon.

All this time George Dupre had been sitting there, his long, thin fingers tapping on the table, while a diamond the size of a .45 slug winked on his left hand. Pa turned to him now.

"Just what are you up to this time, Dupre?"

"Do I have to be up to anything?" Dupre asked, his black eyes cold and deadly.

"That," Pa said, "is like asking a skunk if he smells. You sent your bartender around to coddle up to Pete here by making believe that he was from Massachusetts—which he ain't—and got him over here with a story about apple cider. You got him drunk, probably to pump him about what happened down at the Box Gulch and probably to stuff his fool head with a lot of notions to help you at tomorrow's hearing."

"Drunk . . ." Uncle Pete staggered to his feet again. "I am insulted. I'll have you know that I am a gentleman from

Boston. My folks helped throw the bloody tea in the harbor and—"

"Your folks," Pa cut him off, "came over from Wales— probably in a rowboat. Now set down and keep your trap shut until I find out what Dupre is up to here."

"If you keep talking," Dupre said, "you're apt to wake up in the alley with a broken head."

Pa came slowly to his feet and began to peer around, as though seeking somebody who wasn't at the table.

"And who," he asked flatly, "is going to help you three to do that little job?"

George nodded his head slightly, right and left, and Scofield and Lang came to their feet and out of the corner of my eye I saw the bartender come around the end of the bar with a bung starter in his hands. And then Shagnasty stepped through the bat wings and damned if he didn't have that long-barreled 45–70 in his hands again. When he cocked the hammer you could hear the click of the sear falling home all over the still room. The bartender stopped like he'd run into a brick wall and Scofield and Lang settled slowly and carefully back into their chairs. Shagnasty just stood there, his dark eyes unreadable, his big, sweat-stained hat hanging on his back by its leather thong, his wild hair hanging about his sharply chiseled features.

"Damn you, Shagnasty," Pa said, "go put that damned gun away. We don't need it for this scum."

Shagnasty twitched the long rifle barrel toward the man with the bung starter in his hands.

"Shagnasty think he stay," he said.

"Well," Pa declared, "me and this gentleman from Massachusetts are leaving for the nearest watering trough so that I can see if his head leaks."

And without any further conversation Pa gathered up Uncle Pete and trotted him out the door. As I followed I had a cold feeling between my shoulder blades and wondered if the bartender would throw that bung starter. Perhaps he would have, but Shagnasty kept the rifle on him until I got out and then he turned and followed me. When we hit the street Shagnasty followed and as he passed his horse I saw him shove the big rifle back into the scabbard. Uncle Pete protested every step of the way but Pa hustled him to the Chinese restaurant and sat him down to black, hot coffee.

"Hunt up your mother and Joan," he told me, "and bring them here and I'll buy you all dinner. But take your time about it—I need a little time to get this *Mayflower* hero sober."

I went over to Brannigan's and located Ma and Joan, standing around gossiping with a group of ladies. Since they were in the dress-goods section of the store and I was behind the coffee grinder, they didn't see me. I felt pretty guilty to be standing there, listening to what they were saying, but, after all, Pa had said not to hurry. So I stood there and listened.

"Well," one woman was saying, "the boy could at least have given you time to put on your riding skirt."

"Yes," another said. "I didn't see it, of course, but my husband did. He would—he never misses anything like that. Let a woman's skirt so much as fly up in the wind and he's all eyes."

"I guess it was a sight all right, galloping through town bareback without a riding skirt. You poor girl."

"I don't feel that way about it at all," Joan said crisply. "Tom had only a few minutes to get married in, and if he'd let me take time to put on a riding skirt it might have been too late. Jack Stockman was . . ."

"Alice Hansen," another woman put in, "had to get married in a hurry too. Let's see now. She was married in May and the baby came in October."

"Alice Hansen," Ma said firmly, "was pregnant. My daughter-in-law is not. Why, I doubt if my son had even kissed her."

"Oh, yes he had." Joan's delicious laughter trilled out. "At least three or four times."

Good for you, Joan, I thought. And then I coughed and stepped out to where they could see me.

"Pa and Uncle Pete and Shagnasty," I said, "are over at the restaurant. He sent me to fetch you."

"Good day, ladies," Ma said, and swept out of there with her head high and Joan smiling beside her.

"Damned gossips," I said.

"How do you know?" Joan inquired. "Were you standing there listening to what they have been saying?"

"I was standing," I said, "and when I stand my ears stay open just the same as they do when I ain't standing."

Joan laughed and thrust her arm through mine.

"Pa," I told them, "said not to hurry. It seems that Uncle Pete tangled with some Coyote Wells-style apple cider. Pa wants time to pour black coffee into him before you get there. If he is still tipsy, make believe that you don't notice it."

"Uncle Pete!" Ma exclaimed.

"Yes," I said. "The gentleman from Massachusetts who helped bail out the *Mayflower* when it came over."

"I see," Ma said. "That bad, is it."

"Was," I said. "By now Pa probably has him wide-eyed and bushy-tailed."

When we got to the restaurant Uncle Pete looked awfully subdued and I could imagine that Pa had been riding him for falling for Dupre's little trick. But I didn't have a chance to talk to him because just as we came in, Bill Bullow and his wife joined us and he got lost in the shuffle as we all moved to a larger table.

"Just like I thought," Bullow said after we all got settled and had ordered our food. "Jack Stockman isn't in town and neither is Matt Fillbuster. I'll bet that Fillbuster is looking for him and that Dupre has whisked him out of the country."

While Pa and Bill were discussing this I was making eyes at Joan, and seated where I could look out on the street. First thing I knew, there was Matt Fillbuster riding in, with Stockman riding beside him. Uncle Pete seemed to come alive then.

"Baah Jove!" he exclaimed. "There's Fillbuster and that bleeding outlaw now."

"You're right!" Bill Bullow exclaimed, and we all got up and started down the street toward Fillbuster's office. In passing we dropped Ma and Joan off at the store.

We found Fillbuster locking Stockman up in a cell.

"What did he do?" we asked.

"Nothing in particular," Fillbuster said, "except breathe."

"You haven't any right to lock me up," Stockman raved. "You haven't any proof that I wasn't going to show up at the hearing."

"You wasn't exactly hanging around," Fillbuster said wearily, "when I hauled you off that westbound freight train in Antelope Flats. Anyway, I ain't locking you up for trying to skip the country. I'm locking you up for assaulting an officer."

"I didn't . . ." Stockman sputtered.

"Oh, yes you did," Fillbuster said. "Fought like a wildcat when I tried to get him off that train. Bruised my knuckle something fierce."

And then I noticed that Stockman now had two black eyes.

"Busting up an officer's knuckles," Fillbuster said, and a slow smile came to his lips, "will be enough of an attempted assault on the law to hold this rabbit in a cell until the time for the hearing before Judge Stark. That's the way I look at it, anyway."

"Did you run into Jed?" I asked.

"No," Fillbuster told me, "but another poor devil did. Jed got boozed up in Antelope Flats and shot and killed an unarmed man. I want him now for murder."

CHAPTER FOURTEEN

I don't know when Judge Stark's courtroom started filling up, but it was full of people when we got there at quarter to ten. It seemed that the whole town and half the countryside had turned out to take in the affair. There were, and this was unusual, a lot of women in the audience, probably because of their curiosity concerning Joan's hasty marriage. The benches were all full and chairs had been brought in, and folks were standing, squatting, and practically hanging from the rafters. Town clothes were mingled with riding boots and chaps and men smelling from everything; the odors of cows, horses, sheep, and whiskey were intermingled with the ladies' perfume.

Everywhere was confusion, but somehow Judge Stark's bailiff got everything straightened around. I found myself sitting with Pa at a bench, with Jack Stockman, his lawyer, and George Dupre seated at another bench beside us. Judge Stark looked down at us from his more elevated seat like an avenging angel, his white mustache and tiny, pointed goatee giving him an air of dignity, which was not evident when he started speaking.

"This is a preliminary hearing," he intoned, beating his bench with a bung starter. "It is for the purpose of bringing out the facts concerning what did occur between Jack Stockman and Tom Conway on June fourteenth. Now I'm not going to swear anybody in, but I do want the true facts, not a lot of hogwash."

Everybody clapped.

"John Conway," the judge went on, "do I understand that you are going to act as your son's attorney?"

"You might call it that," Pa said, "but the way I look at it is that I'm just going to spit out the true facts you mentioned."

"I see," Stark said. "Your attitude is commendable, though perhaps unwise. We have a charge here by Jack Stockman that your son, Tom, leaped out of the trees five miles south of town and hit Stockman so forcibly with the barrel of a .45 Colt as to render him unconscious."

"Sage brush," Pa said.

"Eh, what's that?" The judge had a startled look on his face.

"Sage brush," Pa repeated. "My son leaped out'n the sage brush. There wasn't no tree there to leap out of."

George Dupre's lawyer, a short, fat, pudgy individual by the name of Samuel Portly, came to his feet.

"Aha!" he exclaimed. "The defendant does admit that he did leap out at my client and strike him forcibly with a .45 Colt barrel."

Stark banged his bung starter.

"Tom Conway," he stated, "should not be termed a defendant, Mr. Portly, and neither should your client. We are gathered here merely to sort out the facts to see if either person should be held for trial at a later date."

"The best way to get at this here deal," Pa declared, "is for me and Tom to tell our side of it and then for Stockman to tell his side of it. In that way—"

Bang went the bung starter, and the crowd clapped and hooted encouragement to Pa.

"Are you trying," Judge Stark demanded of Pa, aiming his silver goatee at him like a shot arrow, "to tell me how to run my courtroom?"

"No," Pa said, and he gave the judge his best, blue-eyed smile. "You and me is in total agreement, Judge. Now, if this lawyer feller, Mr. Porky, will set down . . ."

"The name," the lawyer said coldly, "is Portly."

Pa looked the man up and down like he was inspecting a prize hog.

"If the shoe fits . . ." he said, and then, "My son admits leaping out of the sage brush and hitting—just how did you hit the snake-in-the-grass, son?"

"Yeah," the judge said. "I never saw a blacker eye in my life."

"I protest," Portly shrieked, leaping to his feet. "The blackness of my client's eye has no bearing whatever . . ."

"Sit down, Mr. Porky—I mean Portly," the judge thundered. "The manner in which your client was hit does have a bearing on this situation, since Tom Conway's guilt or innocence seems to hinge on the matter of intent. Proceed, Mr. Conway."

"Well," Pa said, "Jed Dupre and Steve Holden and this Jackman rattler with the black eye and the busted jaw had us holed up in the old Box Gulch ranch buildings, which Uncle Pete planned on filing on under the Grazing Act—"

"Hold it, hold it," the judge interposed. "Now just who is this man Uncle Pete, and what does he have to do with this matter of leaping out of the sage brush and assaulting . . ."

"Here," a voice came from the audience, and Uncle Pete staggered to his feet and waved a hand. "I'm Uncle Pete."

"This," declared the lawyer who Dupre had brought in from Miles City and who was undoubtedly not acquainted with the Coyote Wells way of doing court business, "is utterly preposterous."

"Ain't it though," Pa said. "The old coot has been at George Dupre's apple cider again, which, to my way of thinking, is interfering with justice."

"Interfering with justice!" the judge said. "In my court? Just what do you mean by that, Mr. Conway?"

"I mean," Pa said distinctly, "that George Dupre has been getting one of my witnesses drunk for two days, with the nefarious purpose of getting him more confused than he usually is, by having his bartender make believe he was from Massachusetts."

"Massachusetts?" the judge queried. "Now what in hell has the state of Massachusetts got to do with your son leaping out of the trees . . . I mean sage brush?"

"The bartender lied," Pa said. "He ain't never been in Massachusetts. Why, he was borned in Antelope Flats—if I recall it, his pa was a sheepherder and his ma . . ."

Samuel Portly leaped to his feet, his usually sonorous voice high and reedy.

"I demand," he yelled, "that this absurd buffoonery be brought to a stop."

"How," Pa complained, "can we get anywhere with this, Judge, if this porky character keeps leaping up and demanding things?"

"You don't demand anything in my court, Mr. Porky—I mean Portly. Sit down while I get to the bottom of this. And you, Uncle Pete, sit down too, until called upon. Now let us confine ourselves to just what Tom Conway did to Jack Stockman, five miles south of town on the morning of June fourteenth, and look into his motivation for doing whatever it was he did actually do."

"You tell him, son," Pa said and sat down.

"Judge," I said, getting to my feet, "I don't see anything mysterious about this. We were camped at the old Box Gulch buildings on Box Gulch Creek after having looked over the section of land they sit on. Since this land was open for filing, we planned on heading back for Coyote Wells in the morning so that my uncle Pete could file on it. But that evening Jed Dupre, Steve Holden, and Jack Stockman here came in and threw down on us with a rifle and a couple of .45s. Jed told us, right out, that since his father wanted the land and wanted to beat us out of it, he was going to hold us there and send Jack Stockman to Coyote Wells to file on it for his father. Stockman turned all our horses loose and choused them off towards town and then lit out for Coyote

Wells with the intention of filing on the land we were after for my uncle."

"And," the judge said, "in some way you were able to follow him and sneak up on him and knock him cold with the barrel of a .45 Colt revolver."

"No," I said, "I knocked him cold with my fist."

"And just how," the judge inquired, "do you account for the fact that you were able to knock a man of Jack Stockman's quite apparent muscular strength cold with one blow of your fist, young man? Are you a trained pugilist?"

"No," Pa declared, coming to his feet again. "The way I get it is that he kneed the bastard in the crotch. You know as well as I do, Judge, that if a feller gets kneed in the crotch he sort of grabs his injured parts and doubles up like, and this causes his chin to stick out so that . . ."

The room rose up and roared and all the ladies blushed. The judge beat his bench with the bung starter and Dupre's lawyer was on his feet with his mouth flapping open but there was so much hooting that I couldn't hear what he was saying.

"I've never," the judge said as the room quieted down, "been kneed in the crotch, Mr. Conway, but I can well understand that this might, as you say, cause a man's chin to be thrust out so that your son might be able to knock him unconscious with one blow. Now, will you explain how your son was able to chase after Stockman and catch up to him when he had no horse—you did say that all horses had been driven away, didn't you?"

"My son's horse," Pa said, "likes him. It wouldn't run off and leave him. It came to him when he managed to get away from Jed's gang, and he rode it bareback into Coyote Wells."

"And," the judge commented, leaning far over and adjusting his glasses to look down at Joan in the audience, "galloped with it down the street here with a lady without a riding skirt—quite a sight, I'm told."

"This is outrageous," Portly sputtered, coming to his feet. But George Dupre motioned for him to sit down.

Dupre stood, tall, carefully dressed, his black hair with the gray sideburns smoothly combed, his dark eyes as cold and direct as the aimed tubes of a shotgun.

"My employee, Jack Stockman," he said distinctly, "has not been afforded the opportunity to present his side of the story—nor has his attorney been offered equal time with Mr. Conway."

"All right," Stark said. "I'm ready to hear his side of it. Mr. Stockman—Mr. Portly."

"My client," Portly stated, "has been employed by George Dupre here for some time—in fact he is a distant cousin of Mr. Dupre. He decided that he wanted to get some land of his own and start his own cattle-raising operation. Not knowing the country, he was guided by Jed Dupre and Steve Holden, who are also employees of George Dupre, to the south, where they decided that the best location for Jack Stockman would be the land on which the old, abandoned Box Gulch ranch buildings stand. They were encamped within these buildings on the evening of June thirteenth when John Conway, Tom Conway, Shagnasty Smith, and Pete Evans descended upon them, armed to the teeth, and engaged them in a fight, during which time Steve Holden was hit in the face with a bench and Jed Dupre was knocked across the room. In the confusion of battle Jack Stockman here managed to escape and dash for Coyote Wells, seeking help from the law."

"That," Pa roared, "is a bedamned lie. Stockman always runs away from the law, not toward it."

"You're out of order, Mr. Conway." The judge banged his bung starter. "Sit down and shut up. Proceed, Mr. Portly."

"My client made his way as rapidly as possible to Coyote Wells and—"

"If he was being so rapid," Pa inquired, "how come he

stopped five miles out of town to build a fire and make coffee?"

Bang went the bung starter, and up went the crowd, encouraging Pa.

"Sit down, Conway. A man can stop for coffee no matter how rapidly he's— There's no merit in your point."

"But there is," Pa insisted. "Stockman dared to take time out because he was the varmint who turned all our horses loose. He dared to take his time because he thought that even if one of us did escape, he wouldn't have ary horse to use to catch up with."

"I see," the judge said. "But proceed, Mr. Portly."

"My client," the lawyer went on, "was fatigued and so was his mount, so he stopped for a few minutes to rest his horse and refresh himself. Tom Conway, in hot pursuit, saw the smoke from his fire and did sneak up on my client with dastardly and evil intent and attack him without warning. He then stole his horse and went on into town."

"Tom never stole no horse," Pa roared.

Bang went the bung starter.

"Sit down, Conway. Now, Mr. Portly, aren't you being a bit unfair in this accusation of horse stealing? It is common knowledge that the horse was released at the edge of town, together with all accouterments attached to it. Now, Tom Conway has admitted attacking your client, and this we all agree on, but we are trying to discover if Tom Conway was in any way justified in making this attack. For if Tom Conway was justified in making the attack, the intent being to delay your client's arrival in Coyote Wells, then he may be justified in temporarily taking possession of the horse. Now let us confine ourselves to whether or not Tom Conway was or was not justified in his attack."

"Now that," Pa declared to the audience, "is what I call plain commonsense talk."

"Sit down, Conway, and shut up. You'll have your opportunity later. Proceed, Mr. Portly. Tell me, did your client attack the Conway group, or did the Conway group attack your client? Call your witnesses."

"He ain't got none," Pa chortled.

"We do have two witnesses," Portly said. "Steve Holden and Jed Dupre. But unfortunately we were unable to contact them in time to get them to this hearing. If the court will allow us more time . . ."

Judge Stark turned his attention now to Pa.

"Since there were supposed to be seven people in the room of the old Box Gulch ranch buildings at the time this attack took place, it seems to me that somebody should be able to come forward and verify who did or did not make this attack."

"I have two witnesses," Pa said. "Shagnasty Smith."

Shagnasty rose from his seat, towering over everybody else, his big hat hanging down his back by its leather thong, his wild hair hatless. He came forward to stand beside Pa, and all his easy, cowboy slouchiness seemed to just fade away from his huge body. He stood straight as a ramrod, tall and proud, with his head up like a thoroughbred stallion scenting the breeze for danger.

"Did you and your friends," the judge asked, "attack Jed Dupre, Steve Holden, and Jack Stockman in the Box Gulch ranch buildings on the evening of June thirteenth, or did they attack your party? Speak up, man."

"Shagnasty," Smith said, his voice low and rumbling but with amazing carrying power, "not savvy big words. But he speak truth. Jed Dupre and two fellers open door, point guns, run off horses. Sprout here, got away—shot in back."

"Sprout?" the judge questioned.

"Tom Conway," Shagnasty said, and his eyes smiled at me. "I call him sprout, ever since he come—little feller with black dog. Little feller then. Big man now. Knock Stockman cuckoo—one punch. Good."

Pa nodded and Shagnasty worked his way back to his

seat. The judge's eyes followed him, his expression thoughtful.

"You have another witness, Mr. Conway?" he asked.

"Yes. Pete Evans. Come down here, Pete."

Uncle Pete made his way down and I could see that although he was not fully recovered from his latest bout with Dupre's cider, he was in comparatively good shape. He had, however, the appearance of a man who was drunk and was determined to appear not to be drunk.

"So," the judge said, "this is Uncle Pete. Question your witness, Mr. Conway."

"Was we attacked or did we attack Jed and his bunch?"

"That," Uncle Pete declared, "is a bloody fool question. Of course we was attacked. Them three bleeding varmints came busting into the room with their guns—the bores of those things looked as big as cannons to me—scared me witless. . . ."

"Then you maintain that you were attacked, Uncle—I mean Pete Evans, that you did not attack?"

"We attacked, all right," Uncle Pete said, "after Tom managed to grab Jed Dupre around the ankles and then make it out the door. Jed shot him along the back. Then Shagnasty Smith booted a bench clean across the room and we attacked, but, Judge, we never did have any guns. Ours were across the room with our saddles and gear."

"I see," Judge Stark said. "Now, several times during this hearing, and the one before it, I have heard suggestions that Jack Stockman was hired by George Dupre to file on the Box Gulch land, and with an agreement to turn the land back to Dupre after he had proved up on it, but I have heard no evidence to substantiate such a charge. Do you have any proof which would make such a charge worthy of being brought to trial before this court? Do you, Mr. Conway?"

George Dupre sprang to his feet.

"Such a charge is ridiculous."

"George Dupre," the lawyer said, "is not on trial here."

"All we know," Pa said, "is that Jed Dupre said that his father wanted the land, and that he, Jed, was sending Stockman to file on it while he held us prisoner. That's all we know, but—"

Bang went the bung starter.

"And Jed Dupre is not here, and apparently can't be found to verify or deny that he said this. So, in the attack by Tom Conway on Jack Stockman, I must rule, in view of the witnesses on one side and the lack of them on the other, that although Stockman was not at the moment holding a gun on Tom Conway, he was part and parcel of a conspiracy to prevent him from reaching Coyote Wells to file on a piece of land that he had chosen, and that therefore Tom Conway was justified in taking action to prevent Stockman from carrying out the conspiracy."

The crowd rose up and cheered, and bang went the bung starter.

"If any of the injured parties," the judge declared when the audience had silenced, "wish to bring charges against Jack Stockman for his participation in this attack on the Conway party, this court will have Sheriff Fillbuster take the proper action to bring these charges before me for trial."

The judge banged his bung starter again and it was all over, and we all went to the Chinese restaurant to eat and to discuss it.

"Next time I get into trouble," Bill Bullow declared, "I'm going to hire you, John, for my lawyer. You did a good job —kneed him in the crotch—that really set up the audience."

"Anyway," Pa said, "we got Tom in the clear. But I thought that the judge should have come down harder on George Dupre hiring Stockman to file for him—he must know that he did."

"Sure he knows it," Bill said, "but he also knows that it would be a waste of time to try to prove it. Stockman would never dare to admit it, with George Dupre sitting right there beside him. The judge has been up against too many cases of this kind not to know the odds. I think that in this case Stark knew all along what the true facts were. The point now is, do you bring charges against Stockman or not?"

"I'm not for that," I said. "He's got two black eyes and a sore jaw for his trouble, and we're going to be too busy from here on out to be bothered with bringing charges against him."

"You can," Bullow said, "if you are willing to pay court costs and hire an attorney and take it to a higher and higher court, because George Dupre would never let it stop with a decision against Stockman on that charge here in Coyote Wells. He wouldn't dare because that would get his neck in the conspiracy noose, too."

"I'm in favor of dropping it where it is," I said.

"Anyway," Pa said, "now that he has no order to appear holding him, I imagine that Dupre will have him out of the country by morning."

"Uncle Pete," I asked, "did you file on the land below or above mine yet?"

"No," Uncle Pete said, backing away from the table. "Let's get right on that now."

So Uncle Pete and I went down to the land office and Uncle Pete filed on the section of land below mine on the Box Gulch Creek. Uncle Pete was going to put up at the hotel, but, remembering the apple cider, I wouldn't go for this.

"The grain bins in the granary are empty now and they are as big as rooms. And then the room where we treat the wheat for smut in the granary can be fixed up with a cot for you, Uncle Pete. You're going home with us. I want to make some kind of a deal with you on us sort of working together on the Box Gulch."

"As far as I'm concerned," Uncle Pete said, "the deal's already made. You got the best cook in the country and I can't cook worth a hill of beans. So if you and Joan will put me up while I'm getting a cabin built on my place, I'll furnish the tools and the grub. You know, before I took up dairy farming I was a carpenter by trade. I reckon, with your help, Tom, that we can fix up your old buildings and build my new one."

"That's more than fair," I said. "Isn't it, Joan?"

"It surely is, and I'd like to have Uncle Pete stay with us —that is, until he gets his house built and finds himself a nice woman to marry."

Joan's eyes were merry and fond on Uncle Pete, and Pete drew out a handkerchief and blew his nose vigorously.

"Me and Ina," he said, "never had any kids of our own. It's going to be nice having you two youngsters around."

I thought so too—that is, as long as I kept a wary eye open for hard apple cider about.

CHAPTER FIFTEEN

After the hearing, Uncle Pete and I began to get ready to move south. Uncle Pete couldn't remember what he had said and done while under the influence of Dupre's apple cider but he could explain why he had boasted about the *Mayflower* and all.

"When I was a kid," he said, "my folks were newly over from Wales and talked with a Welsh accent, and so did I. A lot of folks boasted about their ancestors coming over on the *Mayflower*, or their ancestors tossing the tea in the harbor, or being Boston bluebloods, and I always wished that I could boast about my folks in this way. So I guess when I got lit up with cider it just came out that way. Must have been funny."

"It was," I said.

We were anxious to get south and get our places in some sort of shape before winter set in, but there were many things to do before we could get started. First, I wanted to have a talk with Pa, and my opportunity came when he asked me what sort of a brand I planned to put on my stock.

"Brand?" I said. "Why, I'll use the Boomrang brand, of course."

"The way I figure it," Pa said, "is that half of those heifers we got from Bullow and half that we got from him for wintering his cows last winter belong to you. You'll want a brand on them that will identify them from mine."

"That's not the way I want it, Pa," I said. "I'd like to consider my section on the Box Gulch as just another part of the homestead here, the Boomrang ranch: John Conway and Son is the way I want it."

I wish you could have seen the way Pa's face lit up then, and I knew that he had been worrying about me leaving home—and Ma, too.

"Do you really mean that, boy?"

"Of course," I said. "It couldn't be any other way for you and me and Ma. I've got it all figured out. If I'm not here at harvest time you can hire a hand to do the shocking and drive the bundle wagon at threshing time. Bill Bullow's riders are covering the Bonepile pretty close, now that they have so many cows there—Bill Bullow told me that he'd see to it. Before we drive our stock south from here in late fall we'll round up any stuff you plan to ship out, and load it in the cars for you. With most of our beef down on the Box Gulch you won't have to put up much hay, unless you want to, to winter some more cows for Bullow for part of the calf crop. We'll be working together, hand and glove, Pa, same as always."

"Gad," Pa said, "the Boomrang ranch—John Conway and Son. That has a good sound to it. Folks should have more than one kid, though, so that when one flies the coop there'll be others about."

"I'm not flying the coop. It's just that the Boomrang brand is expanding."

One of the first things we had to do was make sure that Uncle Pete didn't get skinned in buying a wagon and team. I figured on breaking out a team for myself from our range herd but thought that Uncle Pete should have a team that was well broken. We looked around and managed to pick up a team of bays weighing in at about fourteen hundred pounds each, six-year-olds, and a wagon rigged so that we could have bows and a tarpaulin over it in case of rain. First time we went to town, Sam Brannigan told us that Fillbuster had left word that he wanted to see us.

"Shagnasty was just in," Brannigan told us, "and I sent him down. Reckon he's with Fillbuster now."

So we went down to Fillbuster's office to see what it was he wanted. Shagnasty was there and Fillbuster motioned for us to sit down, then carefully lit his pipe before speaking.

"In the excitement of the hearing," he said, "I didn't have time to go into detail about Jed Dupre, and it is important that you know the facts. After Jed and Steve left the Box Gulch they went, as I thought that they would, to Medicine Hills. They started boozing there and from there they went to Antelope Flats. When in Medicine Hills Jed didn't yet know about your marriage to Joan, Tom, and didn't know that you had filed on the Box Gulch section and beaten Stockman into town. But when he got to Antelope Flats the news was there—you know how news travels in this country."

"I know," I said.

"The news that you had married Joan seems to have just about driven Jed batty. He was practically frothing at the mouth, they tell me, and was boasting that he's going to shoot you and make Joan a widow and then marry her. He was doing this in Witherspoon's saloon in Antelope Flats when he ran into Chet Woods, who used to ride for Bullow."

"I know Chet," I said. "A fine fellow—I like him."

"I guess," Fillbuster said, "that he liked you too. Anyway, when Jed got to boasting about what he was going to do to you, Chet called him on it and Jed took a punch at him. There was a fight between the two and Chet knocked Jed down a couple of times. Jed drew and shot Chet in cold blood. Chet was unarmed, and you know what that means."

"It means," Pa said, "that he'll hang if they catch him."

Shagnasty, who had ridden with Chet for many months, growled angrily.

"Chet good man," he said. "My friend—I fix this Jed someday—good."

"You'll have to ketch him first," Fillbuster said. "And now he's really dangerous, because he's got nothing to lose. Kill one man in cold blood and you can't get hung any higher for killing another. The fact that Tom took Jed's girl away from him and married her is driving Jed batty, among other things. I'd not take his boasting lightly if I were you, Tom. I'd take it damned serious."

"Maybe," Pa said hopefully, "George will send him away, out of the country, maybe to South America."

"I wouldn't count on it," Fillbuster said. "Jed will figure that his father is pretty powerful around here and that he'll be safe with him looking out for him. If George backs him, and I think that he will, I'll have a hard time catching up with him. In the meantime, Tom, you take care. If you go south I'd advise you to wear a sidearm at all times."

"Me go with sprout," Shagnasty rumbled. "Jed big trouble."

I guess that we should have paid more attention to what Fillbuster told us but there were so many things to do that we didn't take time out to think much about it. I ran the range horse herd in and roped out a pair of grays, offspring of our stallion Bell Boy, and started riding Chub often to harden him in and break him of his habit of bucking every morning. Chub was a bay with black mane and tail and stockings. He had been accidentally cut a bit proud, so had a little stallion left in him. Filly could outrun him easily, but he was strong and had a lot of endurance. I offered to break in a saddler for Pete but Pa insisted that Pete should have a well-broken cow pony that was gentle.

"Put Pete on anything but a real gentle horse and he'd be on the ground more than he'd be in the saddle," Pa said.

"I don't know about that," Uncle Pete protested. "I'm getting to be a pretty good rider."

"You wait," Pa told him, "until you get after cattle with a trained cow pony; the animal will jump right out from under you."

I thought that it would, too, but figured that Uncle Pete was tough enough to take it until he got the hang of it. But we did get him to buy a nice, well-trained buckskin from Bill Bullow. It is amazing the amount of gear needed for such an expedition, so far away from stores and supplies, especially when this entailed working with wood, which I knew nothing about. But Uncle Pete had his carpenter kit shipped out and knew all about what was necessary, such as axes, saws, wedges, and so forth, to handle wood. I didn't have much money of my own, and Joan wanted to put her money in the pot, and did use some of it to buy warm winter clothing we'd need. I hauled some of our last-year's wheat into town and had it ground into flour at the mill and sacked the bran for feed. So we had all the flour we could use for months.

"You'll want some eggs down there," Ma said, "so get busy and build a cage for them."

"I wasn't thinking of chickens right away," I said.

"How," Joan wanted to know, "am I to make cakes for you without eggs?"

"I'll make a crate," Uncle Pete said. "How big do you want it?"

"A dozen chickens and a rooster will do for a start," Pa said. "But probably the wolves, coons, minks, and cougars will get them before they have time to squat long enough to lay an egg. That's wild country down there and don't you forget it. It may have looked calm and peaceful when we were there, except for Jed and his cronies, but wait until winter comes howling down on you and wild animals get prowling hungry."

"Don't let Pa scare you, Joan," I said. "There isn't anything down there we can't handle with a saddle carbine."

"Better take a sack of corn along," Ma said, "to feed the chickens, and a roll of fencing to make them a run."

"Uncle Pete's wagon," I said, "is sure going to be loaded."

"That's what I got it for," Uncle Pete said, "and those big bays of mine can haul it anywhere, no matter how loaded it is."

Pete was sure proud of those bays.

"And how about butter and milk?" Ma asked. "You're going to need a milk cow, too."

When I rolled my eyes at this they all reminded me of how I had boasted that on my ranch we'd have milk, butter, eggs, and a vegetable garden. Since we were milking only one cow now, we had to look around for one, and finally bought a lanky Holstein which showed a touch of Jersey, from Amos Linder, Grandpa Hobson's lazy son-in-law, who was glad to get rid of her so that he wouldn't have to milk her. I figured that she was long-legged and lanky enough to lead fifty miles and she was fresh and giving a fair pail of milk.

"We don't need to take everything the first trip," I said. "We'll be back here come late fall to gather up the stock for driving down and helping Pa ship to Chicago."

"Yes," Pa said, "but you may not want to bring the wagon back with you."

"We could," I said, "if Shagnasty was along. Uncle Pete could drive the wagon and Shagnasty and I could handle our little bunch of stock on the drive back."

"Shagnasty," Pa said, "works for Bill Bullow. You can't keep borrowing him all the time."

"I'd like," I said, "to hire him to work for me all the time, and I think that he'd do it. But I can't afford to. Bullow pays him thirty dollars a month and furnishes him a cabin and groceries. But later on maybe I could afford to hire him if Bullow would let him go."

"I'd feel better," Pa said, "if Shagnasty was along with you on this trip. You really shouldn't risk taking Joan down there until Fillbuster manages to corral Jed Dupre."

"I've thought about that, but would Joan be any safer here, without me, than she will be down there with me? Jed might try to do something to her here while I wasn't around to protect her."

"Both of you," Joan said, "can just stop talking like that. When Tom goes, I go. Tom isn't scared of Jed Dupre and neither am I. But I wish that I had never gone out with him at all."

Bill Bullow rode over quite often to see how things were shaping up and handed out some good advice now and then.

"Of course," he said, "I haven't seen what shape those buildings are in down there. But from what you tell me it seems like you might be able to chink up the cabin, get some sort of roofs on the barn and tack room. If you take along a few rolls of wire, since there is plenty timber for posts, you should be able to get up enough fence for a small pasture for the milk cow and saddle horses. The horses won't stray once they know where their home place is. Keep close watch on them, though, for a few days. Then, of course, there is Pete's cabin to build."

"Not this fall," I said. "I have a deal with Pete. We board him and he furnishes the grub, and lives with us until we have time to build his cabin and find him a wife."

"Fair enough," Bullow chuckled, "particularly when you've got the best cook around—at least that's what the Prestons tell me."

"Man," Pa said, "you two are going to be busier than a man sacking up wildcats, between now and snowfly, doing just what you have to do down there, let alone coming back here to drive our cattle down come late fall."

"Let's see now," Bill said. "You've got a wagon, pulled by one team, and you're going to lead another team, Pete's buckskin, and a cow. It will look like a parade of pilgrims."

Pa chuckled.

"And," Bill went on, "you have tools, flour in plenty, beans—better let the women check the grub list. Men always leave something out. A man tears his hair when he gets way off somewhere, maybe snowed in, and finds he has flour but no baking powder, salt but no pepper, coffee but no lard. Sure you don't also want to lead a hog along?"

"Wouldn't mind," Uncle Pete said, and he meant it. "Pork chops go mighty good in winter."

"We'll have chops," I said, "but they'll be venison chops. I saw a forked-horn mule buck down there that was fatter'n butter."

"No coal down there," Pa said, "so you'll be chopping wood for the stove and that big fireplace. Your hands will be so blistered from swinging an ax that you won't be able to pull a trigger. But Lordy, would I like to wrap my jaws around some venison steaks. I saw that young buck too, and with him two does and a bigger buck. The big one carried at least five points a side. But mind you, boy, no shooting of antelope—it's agen the law."

"Maybe," Uncle Pete said, winking at me, "we just might get so out of grub we could shoot one legally. Every time I see one of those critters bounding about I get a hungry feeling in my gut."

"They've been making me hungry," I said, "ever since I was twelve years old. But Montana law says no touch unless starving. I don't reckon we'll do much starving with four hundred pounds of flour and a hundred pounds of beans and venison bounding around the cabin."

This sort of talk went on day after day as we prepared to leave, and every day I could see that Joan's enthusiasm for the adventure was growing.

"It's going to be wonderful," she told me. "We'll have our own cabin and our own fireplace—and I simply adore Uncle Pete."

I didn't like to pull out in August, the hottest time of the year, for in Montana this is the time when the water dries up, and even the sage hens stand with their wings out and their beaks open as they gasp for breath. At this time of year we have our only real warm nights. Corn that has grown little all summer may now grow so fast you can almost hear it grow during warm August nights. And yet in early September comes frost. But the days between now and snowfly were precious, so we had no choice but to start out in early August. And this time I was taking my dog, Rover, with us, since Pa's fields were all fenced in and the need for him was no longer great, although he loved to chase the chickens out of the garden with a great flapping of wings and cackling. So, this time I had three of my most loved ones along, Joan, Filly, and Rover. And then, of course, there was Uncle Pete.

CHAPTER SIXTEEN

We got a good break when we started out for the Box Gulch, for although the nights were warm the days were not overly hot. We couldn't make very good time, leading a cow, so we didn't arrive at the Elk Creek camp site until the evening of the second day. The trail was old to me now, of course, but the pleasure of showing it to Joan, her delight in each new mile as it unfolded, made this trip the honeymoon that we had not had after our wedding.

"This," Joan told me many times on the trip, "is the best honeymoon a girl could have."

We traveled slowly over the rolling hills, dry now and pungent with the scent of curing buffalo and other grasses, across saged flats where flocks of sage hens took wing, down into draws and coulees, where cottontail rabbits and grouse lurked, and Joan screamed with delight when graceful antelope bounded away and then signaled to each other with their white rumps that danger was at hand. And Rover, as always indignant over bounding rabbits, had to be put in the wagon finally to keep the poor dog from running himself witless. At noon I taught Joan the art of making a small, hot fire with sage-brush sticks, and the secrets of using the reflector to bake biscuits. Uncle Pete, no doubt realizing that this trip was, to us, a honeymoon, kept largely to himself, driving the wagon, to which were attached my team, his buckskin, and the plodding cow. I rode Filly and Joan rode Lady Bird.

We made a dry camp at noon the first day, and a dry camp that night, giving the animals water from the barrel strapped to the wagon. As evening came down and the long shadows cast by the lowering sun began to steal over the prairie, Joan and I sat on our bedroll and I told her of the lonesome years when I had herded cattle without a horse, with the black and white dog that now lay contentedly beside us. And we talked of Joan's past, and God and Creation, and of how our love had bloomed from the first moment that we met each other. We listened together to the great silence of the evening prairie, until the first coyote of the night sent out its yammering, spine-thrilling call, to be answered by others here and there in the distant ridges. And then we went to bed, secure in our love and in our future together. As Shagnasty was apt to say, "It is good."

We awakened to a cloudless sky and made our hasty breakfast and got under way, traveling steadily until noon, when we rested the horses, ourselves, and the cow for a full two hours. Then we moved on and came down into the inviting shade of the box elders and cottonwoods along the Elk, with the sun still above the horizon.

"Thirty miles in two days isn't bad," Uncle Pete, who knew all about the speed of milking cows, declared.

We took the animals to water, and we lay down and drank from the stream, and Joan insisted on doing this also.

"I'm the wife of a prairie man," she said, "and so I must learn to be a prairie woman."

And I was proud of her, and each day, each hour with her, made me more and more sure that she was right for me, and me for her.

The mosquitoes were not as bad now as they had been in June, for the snow-melt water had largely dried out of the numerous buffalo wallows, where they mostly bred, and Elk Creek still ran fast enough so that there was little stagnant water for their breeding. Joan insisted on taking over at the campfire and did something to canned beans that made them taste better than our beans ever had before, and had her first try at making biscuits with a reflector oven. With dusk hard upon us, and full darkness not far away, while we were eating our meal, I heard an alien sound and turned and there was Shagnasty Smith, standing but a few feet away, looking at us with his big rifle in his hands. Seeing him, I instantly noted that he was not wearing boots and spurs, but beaded Indian moccasins.

"Shagnasty!" I cried out in pleasure, coming to my feet from where we all sat on the ground tarp about our food. "We didn't hear you come up."

"Good!" The big man grunted. "Like fox. Good!"

"Sit down and eat with us. Where's your horse?"

"Big Red over ridge." Shagnasty waved a casual hand toward the west, and then sat down and began to eat prodigiously. Joan's biscuits disappeared as though by magic. He took great, noisy gulps of coffee and smacked his lips over them.

"Better bring Big Red in and picket him out," I said when we had finished.

"Shagnasty," he said, "sleep with Big Red over ridge, sprout."

And as silently as he had come he left, vanishing into the darkness as though he had never been.

"Now," Uncle Pete said in amazement, "what do you make of that? Jumping catfish, has the big fellow gone crazy?"

"No," I said. "Of that I'm sure."

I sat there by the fire in the darkness, watching the dying glow of the coals, and thought about Shagnasty appearing in our camp wearing Indian moccasins instead of his usual riding boots, leaving Big Red over the hill and not bringing his bedroll into our camp. I thought of what this meant and then put my hand in Joan's and asked of her, "Do you really love me, Joan?"

"You know I do," she said softly. "Why should you ask?"

"Because," I said, "if you do, I am the most fortunate of

men, because I have two real loves and that is more than I deserve."

"Two loves?" she queried. "What do you mean by that?"

"I mean," I said, "that big, rough, half-Indian man who just walked out of here loves me, too. He's staying out of sight, guarding us as we travel. God help Jed Dupre if he tries to harm us—Shagnasty will kill him as swiftly as he would a rattlesnake."

I thought then of how Shagnasty had killed that rattlesnake that was poised to strike Uncle Pete, in one fluid, lightninglike motion of the long barrel of his 45–70 rifle. Thinking about it, I involuntarily shuddered, and Joan felt it where her shoulder rested against mine.

"Darling, are you cold—how can you be? It is so warm."

"Not cold," I said. "Just thinking."

Uncle Pete came then with the lighted lantern to drive the darkness away and he and Joan began to clean up the camp while I went and took care of the horses and the cow for the night. And when I laid out our bedroll I laid it as it had been last October, for there was a moon out now, and I wanted Joan to be able to look up through the trees, as I had that fall, and see the moonbeams filtering down through the boughs. I picketed Filly where she could come close to our bed, so that she would be able to awaken me with stamping her fore feet, as she had always done when anything seemed to be wrong at night, such as an animal in camp or approaching riders.

"Does sleeping in the open like this frighten you?" I asked Joan as we got into bed.

"It would scare me half to death," she confessed, "if I were alone. But with you here, big man—poof—who's frightened?"

"The thing to do," I told her, "is like what I used to do when I first started sleeping out on the prairie as a little kid. I sorted out in my mind all the things that could possibly happen during the night, and decided that there was nothing that could happen that I couldn't take care of. There were coyotes, badgers, skunks, gophers, pack rats, none of which would tackle a sleeping man to harm him. There were rattlesnakes, of course, but although I had known of men who had been bitten by rattlesnakes, I had never heard of one being bitten while lying in bed at night on the open prairie. The odds, then, seemed great enough to forget about this too. And then, of course, as a kid I had Rover, even as we have him now beside us. Anything that tries to slip up on us in the night, even one of Pa's pack rats, will be a very sorry animal, believe me."

In the two days that it took to travel from Elk Creek to the Box Gulch ranch buildings we didn't see Shagnasty again, and I realized that he had come into camp that time just to let me know that he was about—the moccasins that he had worn were to indicate to me that he was on a silent scout. Thinking about this, I asked Joan if she'd like to take a little ride with me and told Uncle Pete what we were going to do and that we would join him in a little while again.

"Where are we going?" Joan asked.

"I want to take a look over yonder ridge," I said.

We were now among the stunted cedar and pine growth, and in the August sun their pungent aroma hung in the still air, pleasant to the nostrils, and as we rode, large grasshoppers rose from the grass to fly with a buzzing sound, their wings showing flashes of red when unsheathed in flight. We topped the ridge and pulled up, looking off into endless distance.

"Somewhere off there to the west," I told Joan, "the Tongue and the Big Cougar River flow toward the Yellowstone. And along those rivers the people of Shagnasty's Cheyenne mother roamed and loved and fought, for hundreds of years before the white man came. This country where we ride, Joan, is full of history. Back a way is the town of Medicine Hills, where the tribes gathered to make medicine, for war or peace or maybe just to organize a buffalo hunt. We ride across history, Joan, so see it well so that you will be able to tell your grandchildren about it when it is no longer here, that is, as we know it now."

"Children," she said, her voice soft. "Yes, I'm sure that we will have children. A boy, probably, who will grow up to have an awful temper and will at times swear that his name is Callahan and not Conway."

And then her laughter that I loved so much tinkled out, and I urged Filly forward and down toward the draw below. The sign of the two shod horses of Jed and Steve were still visible, if one looked carefully enough, dimmed by wind and light rain, but still the ground retained the prints of iron shoes. Farther and deeper in the draw, I found what I was looking for and smiled to myself, and Joan, seeing the smile, asked its meaning.

"You said last night," I told her, "that you were a prairie man's wife and so must learn to be like a prairie man. As we rode down here did you note anything of particular interest?"

"What should I have seen that I didn't?"

"You could have seen," I said, "the tracks of Jed and Steve's shod horses, made in June, when I came down here with Pa. The sign is almost gone and you'd have to know it was there and be looking for it to see it. And here, where we are now, an unshod horse passed a short time ago—Big Red —I'd know his hoof marks anywhere."

She looked and when I pointed them out she was delighted.

"I'll learn," she said, "to read sign like an Indian."

"If you do," I said, "you'll have me beat, and you'll have to take lessons from Shagnasty for a long, long time."

"Is there something else I should have seen?" she asked.

"Fortunately, no. I don't see any sign of Jed or Steve or anybody but Shagnasty, sneaking along this ridge. And it would be along this ridge if they were here, for the swell of the land to the east is too far away for anybody to watch us from there. I think that we can be sure that neither Jed nor Steve Holden is hounding our line of travel this time."

"But what is Shagnasty doing here? Why is he acting like this? Why don't he join us in camp?"

"He probably is thinking of Fillbuster's warning about Jed doing us harm, and he is staying out of sight, watching over us. He'll probably follow us all the way to the Box Gulch buildings and once we are safely there he'll probably turn back to go to work again at Bill Bullow's. I doubt if Bill even knows that he is with us. At times Shagnasty can act awfully secretive. Now let's get back to Uncle Pete before he thinks we're lost and begins yelling his head off."

And as we proceeded the timber thickened and grew taller. Then we topped the rise of the land to where it started to slope down toward the Box Gulch. The rise of the land had been gradual, so gradual that one did not notice it, and so was its fall. You couldn't see the fall by looking close at hand but had to look off into distance and gauge the rise and fall over a period of miles.

"We are on the edge of the valley of Box Gulch Creek," I pointed out to Joan. "All the water that falls here, and all the spring snow melt, drains toward Box Gulch Creek, while a few hundred yards back of us the water all drains toward the Elk. So now you are at the very edge of the Box Gulch Creek drainage, of the valley in which you may spend many years of your life; happy ones, I hope."

"I'm sure that they will be," she said.

"But," I warned her, "there will be many times when we will be cold, and maybe hungry, and often we will be so tired that our bones will ache, but we will be where water runs, trees grow to give shade, and where our cattle can graze over many acres. But we won't be able to graze them over countless acres for too many years. Others will come, just like we are coming here, and the country will settle up, but it can never settle up for long too heavily, and the banker in Coyote Wells, Hardwick, gave me the formula for success here, and I'm not about to forget it."

"What do you mean, Tom?"

"I mean," I said, "that those who settle here, as we are doing, on six hundred forty acres, will have just so long to gather their assets together so that they'll have enough funds to buy out those who come later and settle on six hundred forty acres and fail. I saw it happen in Coyote Wells and it will happen here eventually. As Hardwick said, it takes at least four sections to support a family here where rainfall is so scarce. We'll have the creek, and maybe can do some irrigation, but those who later rush down to file on six hundred forty dry acres will fail in most cases, and those who have the money to buy them out, to get the four sections, and more, that Hardwick mentioned, will be the big ranchers of the future here."

"That," Joan declared, "seems a little selfish and hard-hearted to me, Tom."

"I know," I said, "but that is the way it works—I saw it in Coyote Wells. You can't blame Bill Bullow, can you, or fault him, if somebody comes in who is too unprepared, too lazy, or too unwise, and can't make it, if Bill buys their land when it is threatened with foreclosure by land sharks? Bill paid failing settlers for land that they would have lost to mortgages and so got nothing. But what we are talking about now is many years away. When it comes about I'll be dickering for land with white hair and false teeth."

"I can't imagine you with white hair," Joan said.

"Nor I you. But it will come in time, and I'll still be around to see it."

"I hope so," she said, and then, "I'm not sure that I like you so well when you are in one of your serious moods as when you are gay. So let us be gay on our honeymoon and worry about acres and such things later when we are longer married."

"Fine," I said, and almost took her from her saddle, and

she was laughing as we rode down into the valley of Box Gulch Creek.

We came to the place where the land rose sharply into the series of peaks that encircled the buildings to the north and northwest, and topped over where we could look down into the valley beyond. The old log building sat there before the winding stream, with the meadow beyond holding a hint of spring's green, in sharp contrast to the brown hills beyond. And on the meadow a small herd of deer grazed, and I heard Joan gasp as they bounded away.

"It's beautiful!" she cried.

"Yes," I said, "compared to the country we've been riding across it's paradise. But it is also a prime spot for the headquarters of a ranch."

I reached down and pulled my Winchester carbine from its scabbard and rode up beside Uncle Pete on the wagon and motioned toward the shotgun by his side. He grinned and looked at me with that quizzical expression of his, with one rusty eyebrow raised high above the other, as he spat and put the shotgun across his lap.

"What?" Joan asked. "Why the guns?"

"Jed could be down there," I said. "I don't think that he is, but he could be."

"Aren't we ever going to be free of him?" Joan cried out.

"Yes," I said. "I expect that we will in time. But we aren't now. Let's go down, Uncle Pete. Joan, you stay back a ways until we look over those buildings."

Uncle Pete may not have ever driven more than one horse at a time, but he was a natural teamster. He took the wagon down the steep way, with the breeching tight against their hind quarters and his foot braced against the brake lever, and rolled safely into the yard and up to the leaning hitch rack. I swung down from Filly and went through the door, ready for anything, only to be greeted by the big, empty room, with our packs hanging there from the ridge pole, just as we had left them. I made a quick search of the two other rooms and then went to the door and signaled Joan to come on. Uncle Pete came stiffly down from the wagon and then limbered up by dancing a little jig.

"Baah Jove!" he exclaimed. "We made it—slicker'n axle grease. It's hard to believe, Tom, but you and I own two miles of yonder brook."

"Creek," I said. "And we don't own it. Uncle Sam has just lent it to us to see if we've got the guts to live on it for three years. Then, if we make it, he'll arrange for us to own it."

"By damn," Uncle Pete declared, "there's fish in that brook—I mean crick; and what the bleeding difference does it make what you call it; and I'll live here twenty years if necessary to own my mile of it. Did you see that catfish I yanked out of it last time?"

"I not only did see it," I said, "I ate part of it. Now let's get busy and fix this place up for the night."

"Joan," Uncle Pete warned, "ain't going to like sleeping with a slather of pack rats."

Rover had entered the building when I did and was still inside, and as Uncle Pete spoke I heard a scrambling noise followed by a squeaking.

"I don't reckon," I said, "that we'll have much trouble with pack rats with Rover with us. He's got one now. But mice are something else again. Now why didn't we bring along a cat?"

"Baah Jove!" Uncle Pete exclaimed. "I just knew that we'd go and forget something real important."

Joan rode up then and I helped her down and took her into the big living room of the old Box Gulch ranch that had known its days of glory and then seen them fade away after the awful winter of 1886–87.

CHAPTER SEVENTEEN

The first order of business was to get the cabin clean enough for Joan to live in. We all worked together at housecleaning. The old, rusty stove was still in fair condition, and looked pretty good after it was daubed with stove blacking. The rusted iron bedstead was sandpapered and painted white. Joan gave me a real surprise when she produced a feather mattress and two pillows.

"Those," I said, "are full of the down from ducks I shot. Ma shouldn't have given those up. I never saw them loaded in the wagon."

"I know," Joan told me. "She had Uncle Pete sneak them in when you weren't looking. She felt since you shot and picked the ducks that we should have them. And besides, they made the perfect place to carry the panes of glass for the windows, so that they wouldn't get broken."

"Well, I'll be," I said. "I wondered where Uncle Pete packed that glass so it would stand the trip."

So we had a stove and a bed and Uncle Pete made up a bed for himself in one of the bunks in the other bedroom. We swept and scrubbed, hauling water from the creek. We used lye on the planed, plank floor, and Joan cleaned the chimneys of the two bracketed lamps and trimmed their wicks and filled them with kerosene that we had brought along for the purpose.

We chinked up the cracks between the logs of the walls with moss and puttied in the window panes. We axed down trees and made posts and dug postholes and strung wire—

not much, but just enough to contain the horses and the cow until they became accustomed to their new home and until we could enclose a bigger pasture later. The walls still stood on the long, low barn, and the combination blacksmith shop and tack room, but the roofs had caved in. This was the biggest job, to cut and hew out ridge poles for these buildings and other poles for rafters. We didn't expect to get it all done before snow flew, but just enough to cover one end of the barn for our horses and the cow. This barn had once been built to handle a full string of mounts, and the corral, largely in ruins, had been a good one. There was a lot of work to be done there too. As we worked with timber I was amazed at the professional skill of Uncle Pete. He knew every move, from the time a tree fell until it was trimmed and made into whatever he wanted. But with an ax and saw I was as clumsy as a bear cub.

"Baah Jove!" Uncle Pete often exclaimed. "How can you be so clumsy on the ground when you are so good on a horse? I'm feered that you'll cut your leg off with that ax."

Little by little things began to take shape as we worked, the three of us, from dawn until dark. Joan worked wonders with the benches and table, the kitchen shelving, and the tall cabinet with the glass doors. Ma had been wise enough to send along many copies of the Miles City newspaper and sheets from these made the shelves clean and neat. At night, when we came in at dusk, tired to the bone, the big room, with its kerosene lamps, looked as though it had been lived in for years and had never known its years of desertion. Joan was a girl, it seemed, who made a home where she was by merely being there and giving to a place the touch of her hands. Even when utterly worn from work, I found myself completely content. At such times, when I resumed my old habit of always going out to look after the stock before going to bed, I would stand in the warm August darkness, listening to the chuckle of the stream, the contented grazing of the horses, the chirping of the crickets and frogs, scenting in the night air the coming of fall, realizing that soon the mallard ducks would be feeling the urge for their long flight to the south and high overhead would again be heard the talking of the southbound geese. My life, I realized, did not, as with other men, progress by birthdays, from one birthday to another, but from the flight of wild fowl each year. This year, as usual, I would watch and listen to this flight, and have a feeling of being left behind, but this year it would be different, for Joan would be here with me.

During these days of hard work we often talked of Shagnasty Smith, and his appearance at our Elk Creek camp, and of the hoof marks of Big Red over the ridge, undoubtedly moving along with us as we progressed below.

"He probably followed us," Uncle Pete said, "all the way, to see that we got here safely. But why didn't he come down and say hello before he went back to Coyote Wells?"

"Probably," I said, "because he didn't see any use in it. I know how he thinks and acts. He probably looked down and watched me shake out my Winchester and go down and search the buildings and then come out and motion for Joan to come on. Then he probably turned to Big Red—the big guy talks to his horse more than he does to people—and said, 'It good,' and swung up and rode off."

We had been working around the clock for two weeks or more when, in spite of Joan's good cooking, we began to get a yen for fresh meat.

"With meat swimming out there in the brook—I mean crick," Uncle Pete declared as we ate dinner one day, "here we sit, eating bacon and salt pork."

"We ain't sitting much," I said. "It seems to me that we've been on the go every minute."

"Well," Uncle Pete said, "I think that it's about time that we take time off to get some meat. Now down in the brook there's fish a-plenty. Them catfish are good and even them little flat fellers were mighty good fare, once a man got them cleaned. And I ain't too sure that there ain't some trout in that brook. Now if a man would sneak down there this evening after the shadders begin to fall on the water . . . when the shadders fall is the best time for trout—and put a angleworm on the hook . . .''

"Where would you get an angleworm around here?"

"I already got some—found them up by the spring. Got 'em bedded down in wet moss."

"You old scoundrel," I laughed. "You've been planning a fishing trip all along. I'd begun to wonder about that."

"Well," Uncle Pete said, "to you that's a crick down there, but to me it's a brook, and brook or crick, it's fishing water."

"I think," Joan said, "that Uncle Pete has a good idea. We've all been working our fingers to the bone without taking time out to hardly breathe. I haven't really been out of this house since we got here. I'd like to take a walk up the stream while Uncle Pete does his fishing. I want to just walk by the water and maybe sit down and listen to it run—just be plain lazy for a while."

"Well," I said, "I had a mind to take the saddle carbine and go across the field to one of those coulees and shoot me a deer. Now when you talk about fresh meat, it means venison to me."

"No," Joan said. "You can shoot all the deer you want to, and I'll help you eat them, but I don't want to be along when you kill one of the beautiful creatures."

"All right then," I agreed, "we'll take the shotgun and while Uncle Pete goes downstream to fish we'll go upstream and shoot some ducks. I reckon I can bear with a bit of roast duck along with Uncle Pete's fish, if he gets any. We'll leave Rover here to guard the place."

"I'll get some, don't you worry about that. Once the shadders fall . . ."

And so it was settled. We worked on the seemingly endless job of getting some roof over the barn, until, as Uncle Pete put it, the sun got low enough that the banks of the creek began to cast shadows on the nigh bank, and then we laid down our tools.

"Lead me," Uncle Pete yelled, leaping up and cracking his heels, "to them catfish! Here I come."

I went to the house and got the Winchester pump shotgun, shoved six shells into its magazine, and Joan and I started out up the creek. Twice we got up small flocks of mallards, and once two teal winged away from the water, but we didn't get close enough for shooting, and simply because Joan had no idea of how a person should go about it to crawl up on ducks. She was having such a good time just walking along the stream that I hated to criticize her about being cautious. But finally one of the flocks we'd put up circled and began to come back toward us.

"Down," I whispered to Joan, pulling her down with me. "Don't let them see your face—it'll flare them away."

Hunkered down there, watching them out of the corners of my eyes, I waited until I could see, as Pa had told me, the colors, the green heads of the mallard drakes. And then I sprang up, and as they flared, fired three rapid shots. Two birds crumpled and came down, and then with a roar of wings another flock went up from close at hand, that had been hidden from us by the creek bank. Hearing them, I spun around and fired three more shots, so fast that I pumped and pulled once on the empty gun, hearing the hammer click down on the empty chamber, and three more ducks floated there on the water. And then I heard Jed Dupre's heavy voice behind me.

"Hold it right there," he said, "or I'll blow your honyoker head off."

He circled around, to get between me and the creek, his saddle carbine at full cock, held ready, and looking at him I felt like a fool to be caught like this. He had been wise enough to wait until we felt secure.

"What took you so long, Jed?" I asked. "We were expecting you earlier."

"I knew you were," he said. "I ain't the fool you take me for."

"You can't get away with this," I said. "Besides, I don't see any point to it. What do you want? What are you after?"

I glanced aside to see Joan standing there, her eyes shocked, a hand across her lips.

It was then that I began to think that Jed Dupre was actually mad, for the most ferocious expression came to his face and his eyes glittered with the hatred behind them.

"What do I want?" he echoed, and he threw back his head and his laughter was a hideous thing. "What do I want? What have I always wanted?"

He pointed a finger trembling with rage at Joan.

"Her," he said flatly. "She's what I wanted, and you took her from me, and for that, Tom Conway, I'm going to kill you."

"You'll have to," I said, "before I'll let you touch her."

"I'd planned on it," he said.

"They'll hang you if you do that."

"You damned fool," he spat out. "They can't hang me twice. I fixed that Chet Woods in Antelope Flats, just like I'm going to fix you."

"And then what?" I asked.

"Then I'm going to grab little Miss Double Crosser here and leave the country. Oh, my dad has got it all arranged. Nobody will be able to stop me. Now get down on your knees and pray, honyoker."

And then the rifle came up and centered on my chest and I was looking right down the barrel and into Jed's eyes, seeing the madness in them. Joan screamed and flung herself at him, but he swept her aside with a lash of the rifle barrel and she fell and lay still. I followed her leap but as she fell she tripped me and I went rolling, coming to my feet. But Jed had backed away now, rifle held ready.

"For God's sake, Joan," I cried out, "stay where you are. Don't move."

I didn't know if she was conscious or not, but she didn't move. I had the thought that if I could stall Jed a few minutes perhaps Uncle Pete would come upstream to see how many ducks we had gotten, for although he was too far away to hear our talking, he must have been near enough to hear the bellow of my shotgun. But knowing how intent Uncle Pete was on his fishing, it seemed that there was little chance for help from him. But just in case, I started trying to delay Jed with my talk, to gain time, hoping for a break of some kind.

"You won't gain anything by this," I said. "Joan hates your guts. She won't go with you willingly, and if you force her she'll hate you even more. A woman is no good to a man if she don't love him."

"Shut up!" he screamed, and then I saw froth at the corners of his mouth. And then I saw something else over his shoulder. I saw Big Red appear on the rim of the hills, and Shagnasty swing down from him. I averted my eyes so that Jed would not see something in them that would warn him. Shagnasty stood there like he was looking intently, and I expected him to leap back on Big Red and come galloping and shouting to my rescue. I knew that if he did this I would be a dead man. Jed would shoot instantly. I knew this just as certainly as I knew that the sun would rise in the morning. Jed would shoot, and grab Joan and run. Shagnasty would run him down and rescue Joan, but I would be dead.

But Shagnasty was not getting back up on Big Red. I saw him yank the big rifle from the saddle and fling it up, aiming toward us. My God, I thought, surely he isn't going to shoot. In spite of Shagnasty's boasting about "shooting in the ear at half mile," I knew that the 45–70, single-shot government rifle was really a short-ranging weapon. Its heavy slug, driven by black powder, was not of much good beyond two hundred yards, and Shagnasty stood at least four hundred yards distant. If he shoots, I thought, I'm dead.

But it certainly looked as though he was going to shoot, for he stood like a graven image with the long rifle pointed toward where we stood. Jed's back was toward Shagnasty, so he could not see him, but I was afraid that he would see something in my eyes, or sense Shagnasty's presence.

"Down on your knees, sodbuster," Jed said, "and beg— I'm going to blow your damned head off."

And then I saw Shagnasty's shoulder jerk back, and saw the puff of black powder smoke at the barrel's end. After what seemed a long second I heard the heavy ball strike Jed between the shoulders and drive him face down on the ground while the bullet from his rifle gouted sand up in my face from between my feet. And then I was leaping forward, wrenching the rifle away, turning Joan over, looking down into her frightened eyes.

"Tom," she moaned. "Oh, Tom. Are you hurt?"

And I could hear the tattoo of Big Red's hooves as the big horse thundered across the meadow, lunged through the stream, charged up the bank, and was hauled up short as Shagnasty hit the ground, reddish-black hair and whiskers a tangled mass, dark, piercing eyes ablaze with the fever of battle. He nudged one huge moccasin under Jed's shoulder, rolled him over, and stood there, looking down at him there on the ground, and then he turned and looked at us and the battle light went away from his eyes, and a great warmth came to his features.

"This one," he said, nodding down at Jed's body, "no more trouble to sprout and little lady. Good!"

"My God, Shagnasty," I cried out. "We thought you were back at Coyote Wells. How did you happen to be here?"

"Shagnasty camp in hills. Long time. Shagnasty know this one come sometime. Me watch. Me wait."

"But how could you hit him from so far away?"

Shagnasty shrugged his shoulders.

"Shagnasty," he said, "hold a little bit high, little to side for breeze. Someday Shagnasty teach sprout how to shoot."

He turned to look down again at Jed.

"Him dead," he said matter-of-factly. "Good."

Him was dead, and I took Joan away, shielding her from seeing the body, and I took her back to the cabin and put her on the bed and examined her wound. There was a swelling and black-and-blue spot on the side of her head along the cheekbone.

"I'll heat some water," I said.

She wasn't crying or having hysterics but she seemed to be shocked speechless. But now she cried out.

"No!"

"It's all over, Joan," I said soothingly. "Jed won't ever bother us again."

"No!" she cried out again. "Go take him away. I don't want to see him. Take him away."

So I went out and met Shagnasty walking across the yard with a shovel in his hands.

"What are you going to do, Shagnasty?" I asked.

"Bury he," he said.

"No. You mustn't. We'll have to tie him on a horse and take him into Coyote Wells to Fillbuster."

"Why?"

"It's the law. There will have to be an inquest."

"Law." Shagnasty's words were scornful. "Law no help you. Shagnasty help you. Shagnasty shoot. Shagnasty bury. If law want to dig up . . ."

He shrugged his heavy shoulders and went plodding over to mount Big Red and I stood there and watched him ride out. Yes, the law could dig up if they wanted to, and probably would. If they didn't want to— I too shrugged my shoulders.

I stood there and watched Shagnasty load the body on Big Red and start away with it, and wondered if he'd changed his mind, and then it came to me what a man like Shagnasty, my best friend on earth, would do. When he came back a half hour later, after I had put hot packs on the side of Joan's face, I knew that I had guessed right.

"Bury he," he said, "off sprout's land. Let law dig there, not here. Little lady no want here. Me go now, see Fill-buster."

And then he swung up on Big Red, lifted a hand in fare-well, and I just stood there and let him go, not knowing what else to do. Knowing that this was the way he would want it. I could pour out words of thanks and it would only embarrass him, this big man who had followed us all the way from Coyote Wells and had the Indian patience to slink about in the hills for more than two weeks, waiting for the time that his instincts told him would surely come. Jed Dupre was sly, as Fillbuster had said, but Shagnasty Smith was even more crafty and sly. Did any man, I asked myself, have such a friend as this? Everything I owned now, and everything I would ever own, I owed to this man that many far lesser men looked down upon as the half-breed offspring of a beaver trapper and an Indian woman—I wouldn't call such a woman squaw, even in my thoughts. As I stood there in thankfulness, Uncle Pete came, carrying some catfish and some ducks.

"What was all the shooting about and why didn't you pick up your ducks? These here come floating by and I jumped in and got them out."

I noticed then that Uncle Pete was all wet, from heels to reddish hair.

"A man shoots ducks," he complained, "he should jump in and fetch them out himself. That water's bloody cold, let me tell you."

"You better clean those fish at the creek," I said. "Joan won't want them cleaned in the kitchen."

Uncle Pete turned away toward the creek, some of the light going away from his kindly, friendly features, because

I had not made a fuss over his catch of catfish. And then I went back to Joan. Yes, Fillbuster would come, and maybe he would dig, and carry the body away, and I would have to write down all about just how it had happened, and swear to it over my signature, and then it would be all over. Then we could live in peace in the valley of the Box Gulch, and perhaps, as Joan had said, raise a lad with a quick temper who would, at times, swear that his name was Callahan and not Conway. And the thought warmed me as I went in to comfort Joan, as I hoped to comfort her for as long as we both lived, working together to build up the Boomrang brand of Conway and Son.